I Am America

STRANGER ON THE HOME FRONT

A Story of Indian Immigrants and World War I

Book design by Jake Slavik
Illustrations by Eric Freeberg

Photographs ©: Shutterstock Images, 144, 145 (top), 145 (bottom); North Star Editions, 146–147

Published in the United States by Jolly Fish Press, an imprint of North Star Editions, Inc.

First Edition
First Printing, 2020

This is a work of fiction. Names, characters, places, and incidents are either the product of the author's imagination or are used fictitiously, and any resemblance to actual persons living or dead, business establishments, events, or locales is entirely coincidental.

Library of Congress Cataloging-in-Publication Data
Names: Chhabra, Maya, author. | Freeberg, Eric, illustrator.
Title: Stranger on the home front : a story of Indian immigrants and World War I / by Maya Chhabra ; illustrated by Eric Freeberg.
Description: First edition. | Mendota Heights, Minnesota : Jolly Fish Press, [2021] | Series: I am America | Summary: Living in California in 1916, Margaret Singh thinks nothing of the war in Europe or the cause of Indian independence until the United States enters the war, her father is arrested, and her own allegiances are called into question. Includes author's note.
Identifiers: LCCN 2020002969 (print) | LCCN 2020002970 (ebook) | ISBN 9781631634864 (hardcover) | ISBN 9781631634871 (paperback) | ISBN 9781631634888 (ebook)
Subjects: CYAC: Parent and child–Fiction. | Loyalty–Fiction. | East Indian Americans–Fiction. | World War, 1914-1918–United States–Fiction. | India–History–British occupation, 1765-1947–Fiction. | LCGFT: Historical fiction. | Fiction.
Classification: LCC PZ7.1.C49775 St 2021 (print) | LCC PZ7.1.C49775 (ebook) | DDC [Fic]–dc23
LC record available at https://lccn.loc.gov/2020002969
LC ebook record available at https://lccn.loc.gov/2020002970

Jolly Fish Press
North Star Editions, Inc.
2297 Waters Drive
Mendota Heights, MN 55120
www.jollyfishpress.com

Printed in the United States of America

I Am America

STRANGER ON THE HOME FRONT

A Story of Indian Immigrants and World War I

By Maya Chhabra

Illustrated by Eric Freeberg

Consultant: Rajan Gill, Professor of History, Yuba College

Mendota Heights, Minnesota

A Note on Vocabulary

India, at the time this story is set, included modern-day India, Pakistan, and Bangladesh. The entire area was ruled by the British Empire and sometimes referred to as **Hindustan**.

Punjab was a region within Hindustan (now partly in India, partly in Pakistan). Most Indian immigrants to the United States at the turn of the century came from this region. Punjabis could be of any religion, with the three main religions of the region being Islam (whose followers are called **Muslims**), Sikhism, and Hinduism. **Lahore**, in present-day Pakistan, is a major city in Punjab.

Sikhism is a religion that started in the 1400s in Punjab. Most early Indian immigrants were **Sikhs**. Many Sikhs use the last name Singh, which means "lion." Many wear **turbans** to cover their long, uncut hair. The **kirpan** is a knife worn by many Sikhs as a symbol of their faith.

A **gurdwara** is a Sikh house of worship. The first gurdwara in the United States was in Stockton, California. **Langar** is the common meal prepared at the gurdwara for all worshippers and visitors. **Phulka** is a flatbread common in Indian food. It is more often known as chapati.

The **Golden Temple** in the Punjabi city of Amritsar (in modern-day India) is the holiest site in Sikhism. **Guru Nanak Gurpurab** is a Sikh holiday celebrating the birth of Guru Nanak, who founded the religion. The **Guru Granth Sahib** is the Sikh holy book.

Hindus are followers of the majority religion in India. Though many early twentieth-century immigrants to the United States were Sikhs or Muslims, Americans called them all Hindus or **East Indians** to distinguish them from American Indians/Native Americans.

The **Ghadar Party** was a revolutionary group founded by Indian immigrants. Members planned to use violence to end British rule over India. The word *Ghadar* means revolt or mutiny and was sometimes spelled "**Gadar**."

The Immigration Act of 1917 banned most immigration from Asia to the United States. It was informally called the **Barred Zone Act**.

During World War I, Germans and particularly German soldiers were called **the Huns** in the United States and other Allied countries. The **kaiser** was the emperor of Germany. **U-boats** were German submarines. **Prussia** was the largest state in Germany and included the capital, **Berlin**. The **Berlin-India Committee** was an organization of Indian revolutionaries working with the German government during World War I.

LAHORE, PUNJAB

November 16, 1915

MUTINY FAILS, ORGANIZERS EXECUTED

After being sentenced to death in September, nineteen-year-old Kartar Singh Sarabha was hanged along with six others in the city of Lahore in November. Sarabha had been arrested in Punjab, India, for trying to incite mutiny among Indian soldiers and convince them to turn their weapons against Britain. Sarabha had recently returned to India from the United States, along with numerous other revolutionaries. The revolutionaries were acting on behalf of the Ghadar Party, a group based in California. It is thought that the gurdwara in Stockton, California, may have provided them with financial support.

Chapter 1

Autumn 1916

Margaret Singh and her family were late, as usual. They came to Stockton from San Francisco every year for the festival, and every year they got lost somewhere between the train station and the gurdwara. Margaret's stomach rumbled, but there wouldn't be any food till they got there.

Father stopped a couple of passersby to ask for directions. "Excuse me, do you know where the Sikh temple is?"

One of the strangers looked like he was going to say something impatient, but then he caught sight of Margaret and Mother. He looked at them curiously, as if putting two and two together—Father, the clean-shaven East Indian, wearing a hat rather than a turban; Mother, the white woman; and Margaret, their daughter. Margaret had watched people go through this process a thousand times. A man from India with a white wife was an unusual sight in California. She held her breath. No one here in Stockton knew them, and one never knew how strangers would react.

"You want the building where all the Hindus are meeting?" he asked. "Just keep going straight, then take a left and another left."

They thanked him, but as they resumed walking, Margaret heard him say to his companion, "These Hindus don't even know where their own meeting is."

Father's face fell, and he and Mother exchanged a knowing look. The man had given them the right directions, though, and soon they arrived at the familiar wooden building with tall stairs on either side leading to a second-floor landing and a massive sign over the gable reading "Sikh Temple."

"Ranjit!" A man came out to meet them. He clearly recognized her family, but Margaret couldn't remember who he was. "Late, but still in time for langar, as usual. Come in and have something to eat. Ah, and you've brought your family! Alice, lovely to see you again. And Margaret, you've grown taller! How old are you now?"

She still couldn't remember what his name was, though he knew her whole family. Fortunately, most of Father's friends were happy to be called "uncle."

"I'll be twelve next year, uncle," she said, smiling to cover up her confusion. Just then, her stomach made a loud and embarrassing demand for food.

"Come in and eat something," the man repeated, and they didn't hesitate.

There was no meat in the meal—so that vegetarians could eat too, Father said—but it was tasty. They sat on the floor to eat it. They mostly ate with their hands, but after last year, when she'd made a mess of her new dress, Margaret couldn't help but wish for a knife and fork. This time, she ate slowly and cautiously, scooping up little bits of vegetable curry with the phulka.

Margaret quickly grew bored by the grown-up talk, which was mostly in Punjabi anyway. There weren't any other children there, except for one two-year-old who kept trying to run off. He was too young to be much fun, and besides, if she showed any interest in amusing him, she'd probably find herself watching him for the rest of the day, the way her friend Bettina was often stuck making sure her three-year-old brother didn't get into trouble. That definitely wasn't her idea of a fun festival day.

Looking up, she noticed that Father had left, and Mother was looking around for him. Margaret started scanning the room as well. She spotted a few men with short hair, but none of them was Father.

Maybe he'd gone outside. She slipped out onto the second-floor landing and heard voices. Peering over the railing, she saw a small group of men talking below her. They stood to the side of the first-floor entrance, almost concealed by one of the outside staircases. She could see the tops of their heads from above, and the large turbans most wore. Father was among them. A gust of cold autumn air made her shiver, and she wondered why they didn't come in.

"The British have been on the lookout for the last few years, and the *Annie Larsen* getting caught with arms aboard didn't help," one of the men was saying.

Margaret had never heard of this ship, but it sounded like they were talking about the war between Britain and Germany. More grown-up talk, but at least it was more interesting than the women discussing who'd met their husband when. Without really intending to eavesdrop, she lingered a little away from the men, trying to hear—all right, she was eavesdropping.

So was another person, as far as Margaret could tell. Opposite her on the landing, and standing a few steps down, a man looked down at the group. She stared, wondering why he lingered rather than joining in. When he saw her looking at him, he turned around and went back inside.

Margaret had lost the thread of the conversation, but then she heard Father's name.

"Ranjit, we're very glad of your contributions," the man who'd mentioned the ship was saying. He looked younger than her father, as best as she could tell from above, and his suit was immaculate.

Contributions to what? Margaret wondered. *To the gurdwara? To a charitable society?*

"It's not much," Father said modestly.

"It's more than most of our members can afford," another man said.

"I'm lucky enough to run a store in the city. Most of the others are laborers and farmers. It's the least I can do."

"You have a wife and child here, though. Most men who do give that as an excuse to stay out of politics. And your wife isn't one of us."

"Having a family here is just another way I'm lucky," Father said softly. Margaret knew most of his friends had either left their families behind in India or were bachelors. It was hard for Indian women to come to America because of the immigration laws, and only a few of the men had recently been able to marry here. Father was right—Margaret's parents were extremely lucky.

"Besides," Father continued, "now that you have backers in Germany, the Ghadar Party will hardly be as dependent on our contributions. The Berlin-India Committee is very well connected."

Things started to click in Margaret's head—the ship with weapons, the German money, the party contributions.

She shuddered, and not because of the wind picking up. What was Father involved in?

"We have to be careful, though," a tall man closer to Father's age said, looking around nervously. "Working with Germany is treason to Britain. People have already been executed for it in India. Even a boy from around here, a student who sailed back home."

"I heard all about that poor young man," Father said, shaking his head. Then, more confidently, he added, "But don't worry, America's neutral territory. There's nothing the British can do to us here."

Margaret stood petrified in the shadows. The war in Europe had been going on for two years now, and she'd heard all about the crimes of the kaiser, the ruler of Germany, who'd sunk passenger ships and invaded Belgium and France. People even said America might go to war with him too. But here Father was talking about working with the Germans, taking money from them! She should never have come outside to listen.

"Who's there?" Father called out suddenly, looking up and scanning the staircase. The tall man nearly jumped out of his skin, but the younger man in the neat suit stayed calm.

Margaret's heart pounded. She knew they'd seen her. And there was more at stake here than just having eavesdropped on adults. She had heard secrets about the war.

"M-mother is looking for you," she stammered, the first thing that came to mind.

"Ah, it's my daughter," Father reassured the other men. He broke away from them and climbed the stairs to join her.

"How long have you been out here?" he asked, wrapping an arm around her shoulders and guiding her back inside.

"Just a moment," Margaret lied, smiling. "You startled me."

~

They stayed the night at the farmhouse of one of Father's friends, who had some land along the river. Margaret watched the water glitter with the light of the full moon that announced the festival of Guru Nanak Gurpurab. Because they only came for the holiday, Stockton was always bathed in chilly moonlight in her mind.

She wrapped her shawl tighter around herself. She didn't know that much about Father's religion, or his homeland, or even, she was realizing, what he was involved in now. From what she'd overheard, it sounded dangerous. They'd talked about a ship with arms, and a man who'd been hanged.

"Margaret!" Father's voice came from across the field. She saw him walking toward her. "Oh, so that's where you've gotten to. Be careful around the river. Come on inside. It's time you were asleep. We have to catch an early train tomorrow."

She sighed and turned away from the hypnotizing play of light on the water's surface. If only she could turn away from the thoughts racing through her mind as easily.

"What's gotten into you?" Father asked. "Something's bothering you, I know it. It's not like you to be this solemn."

Margaret tried to hold it all in, the fears and doubts that had been dogging her since she'd listened to the men outside the gurdwara. But she couldn't. Even if she got in trouble for eavesdropping, she had to know.

"I heard you talking at the gurdwara today. About the British and the Germans and arms and—and someone being executed." Her throat was closing up, and it was hard to talk. "Father, what's going on?" she choked out.

Father looked around suddenly, even though there was nobody nearby. Then he looked at her very seriously. "You know about how India is part of the British Empire?"

She nodded. She'd heard him say bad things about the British before.

"They don't rule it very well, right?" she asked when she could breathe properly again. "But what does that have to do with—"

"It's much worse than them not ruling India very well, Margaret. I haven't told you very much about it, which is my fault. The British came to trade at first, but soon they had their own armies and were in charge. Now India is under the British Crown, and even the regions that they say run themselves have to do what the British tell them. The highest officials are always British, and we have no say in how our country is governed. The British lord it over the people, and the worst part is that we let them. I was even in their army for a while. I volunteered! It was better pay than farming, and I didn't see anything wrong with it then."

His voice trembled with anger. Margaret had never heard him talk so much about his homeland, and certainly not so passionately. But one thing didn't make sense to her.

"Why would you join the army, if the way the British treat you is so bad?" she asked. Why would her father work for the people who had taken over his country?

Father sighed. "I didn't always realize how bad it was. And even when I did—when I saw the high taxes that make Britain rich, while many in India go hungry, or how a British person can insult an Indian and the Indian just has to let it happen—I didn't see how things could be any different. I thought it was just the way things were. Then I came here."

Margaret struggled for something to say. What Father had told her about India was sad, but surely there was a happy ending to the story. He had come to a better place, hadn't he?

"Because here we have democracy and things, right?" she asked. "And no one tells us what to do."

"That's not what I realized," Father said, pacing back and forth on the riverbank. "America has high ideals. It says all men are created equal, and I believe that too, but that's not how I was treated when I came here. I worked hard and followed the law, but even here, I could never be equal to white Americans, never be respected."

He turned to face Margaret. "That's when I realized that as long as my country was downtrodden, no one would respect me, even outside the British Empire. When India is free, it will be different."

Father fell silent. Margaret picked nervously at a loose thread on her shawl. She was thinking about the man who'd given them directions earlier, and how he'd insulted Father before they were even out of earshot. Could it really be that if things changed in India, people would treat her family better here in America? India was so far away, a long journey by steamship; she'd never been there and probably never would.

"But what can you do from here?" she asked. "And what does the kaiser have to do with it? I heard you talking about Germany."

Father wagged his finger teasingly. "Who taught you to listen to other people's conversations? Certainly not your mother and me." Then he sobered and shook his head. He held out a hand to her, which she took, and they started walking toward the lights of the farmhouse. "Listen, Margaret, you can't ever tell anyone what you heard today. Pretend it never happened."

"I will," she promised. Then she burst out, "But I don't even understand it myself!"

"Keep your voice down!" he said urgently, his hand tightening around hers as he stopped in his tracks. "All right, I'll explain. Britain and Germany have been at war for two years, and the war isn't just in Europe. It's in Africa, it's in the Ottoman Empire, it's all over the world. Indian soldiers serve Britain, just like I used to—thousands and thousands of them. If we could just get those soldiers to turn their guns against the British, then India would soon be free. Of course, the kaiser would be happy to weaken Britain as well, so he helps us—"

"Us?" she interrupted. It was one thing to know her father had been a soldier once, another to hear him talk of guns and war and the kaiser.

"The Ghadar Party. The party of revolt. We believe that only force can drive out the British."

Margaret's eyes grew wide. Father was taking an awful risk. "But they'll hang you if you're caught! Like that student you were talking about."

To her surprise, Father laughed. "The British can't reach us here. We're nowhere near India. And America isn't even in the war, so there's no treason to this country. America fought against Britain for independence, and that's no different from what we're doing. We're not in danger here."

But he looked around the empty field again, and out over the water, as if wanting to make sure they were alone. "Come on, let's go inside. It's late."

"Father?" The way he'd scanned their surroundings made her remember the man on the staircase of the gurdwara.

"Yes?"

"Do you think someone could have been spying on you?"

"Besides you?" Father teased.

"That's not what I meant." Margaret tugged on his hand earnestly. "I saw a man who I think was listening in. He went inside when I looked at him. He seemed . . . I don't know. Sneaky." What if he'd known what the men were talking about, and didn't like it? What if he'd come out on purpose to spy on them?

Father's hand tensed in hers, then relaxed. "I'm sure it was nothing. But I'll tell the others, just in case. And Margaret?"

"Yes?"

"Keep this to yourself."

~

Margaret slept badly. The farmhouse was too quiet compared to the bustle that never died down back home in San Francisco. She hadn't realized that too little noise could be as disturbing as too much of it. She tossed and turned all night as if she had a stomachache, but it wasn't food she was trying to digest. It was everything Father had told her.

He said that there was no danger here in the United States, but was that true? And how could her mild-mannered father be involved in something so radical and risky? What else was he hiding from her?

Every time Margaret opened her eyes, it was still dark as pitch outside. Morning couldn't possibly take this long to come. Eventually, she drifted off, too tired to keep up with the thoughts racing in circles through her mind.

In her dreams, she was following the lurking man she'd seen earlier. He twisted through the streets of Stockton, sneaking around corners and cutting behind buildings. She was so busy trying to keep him in sight that she didn't notice where he was leading. Soon she found herself in a dark alley and, panicking, realized she couldn't find her way back to the gurdwara at all. She turned around, trying to retrace her steps, but as soon as she did so, she felt a heavy hand on her shoulder.

"Curiosity killed the cat," a sinister voice whispered. "I could see you from a mile off." The hand jerked her around, pulling her back into the shadows, and—

She jolted awake and sat bolt upright, trying to catch her breath.

After that, she didn't even try to sleep, just waited for the first tendrils of sunlight to come in the window.

Chapter 2

Spring 1917

History class was Margaret's favorite. It was much better than math, where she was near the bottom of the class, or German, where no matter how much she studied, she couldn't catch up to Bettina, whose father was from Germany. Everyone said German class might be replaced by French or Spanish soon, because of the war in Europe, and as far as Margaret was concerned, that couldn't happen soon enough.

Today, Miss Taylor was lecturing on the American Revolution. "And who can tell us where the first battle of the War of Independence was fought?"

Margaret's hand shot up. "Lexington and Concord, ma'am, in Massachusetts."

"Very good, Margaret. Many of the fighters on the American side were minutemen, ordinary men who had to be ready at a minute's notice to go fight. They needed to be alerted before they could assemble. Today, you'll learn about Paul Revere's famous midnight ride, made immortal in the Longfellow poem 'Paul Revere's Ride,' which you should all memorize by the day after tomorrow. Revere warned the people that the British troops were on their way."

Father had talked about the American Revolution too. He'd said there was no difference between India seeking its freedom from Britain and America doing the same. Margaret imagined her father as a minuteman, carrying a musket, ready to fight the British. After all, he'd told her that he'd been a soldier once.

"Hello, Margaret? Are you there?"

Margaret looked up. Her best friend, Bettina Schmidt, was standing next to her. As she watched, Bettina started to repin her messy hair into a bun. Her blond curls tended to fly everywhere, no matter how carefully she put them up. "It's time for lunch," Bettina said. "Come on."

They grabbed their school's offering of baked beans and bread, then sat outside in the schoolyard. Bettina ate quickly, talking with her mouth full, while Margaret took dainty bites.

"You've been acting funny ever since you got back from that festival, and it's been months," Bettina said. "Did they bewitch you at the temple or something?"

Margaret winced a little inside. People always acted like there was something dangerous about Indian religions. The truth was that there wasn't anything sinister about the gurdwara—unless you counted the plotting she'd overheard. She wished she could tell Bettina what had really happened. Maybe Bettina would be excited to hear about the plot—it was like something out of one of the adventure novels she always had her head buried in. And it had to do with Germany, where her father was from. But Margaret had sworn to keep it a secret.

She took a big spoonful of beans to buy time and to catch up with Bettina, who had already finished eating and was getting restless, looking around the open space for something to do.

"Anyway," Bettina said, "there's a new girl in class, did you notice? Agnes Fitzgerald. She's sitting over there. Let's go say hello."

Margaret swallowed and followed Bettina over to a small group clustered around a petite girl with auburn hair. The girl, who must have been Agnes, stayed seated as she accepted the other students' attention, as if she were a queen and the others her subjects.

"Who's that?" Agnes asked as they approached. She did not seem particularly shy or nervous for someone who didn't know anybody there.

Bettina introduced them. "I'm Bettina, and this is my friend Margaret Singh. How are you liking San Francisco?"

"Pleased to meet you." Agnes didn't look too pleased, though. "They let just anyone into the white schools here, don't they?"

Margaret seethed. Agnes had to mean her. Margaret was by far the darkest-skinned student in the school, even though there was one Japanese student a few grades down, and she saw people even darker than her every day on the streets of the city. They had to go to separate schools, though. There were run-down schools for black students and the Oriental Public School for the Chinese. Margaret had almost had to go to the Oriental School, but her mother had begged the principal of the public school to admit her as a favor. Everyone knew that the white schools got the most money and the best supplies.

"Don't you talk about Margaret that way!" Bettina was red in the face. "She belongs here more than you do."

The rest of the girls were either gawking openly or moving away. One of those remaining, Minnie, said, "Calm down, Bettina. She's just asking." Minnie didn't say anything to Margaret at all, like it had nothing to do with her.

Margaret shifted back and forth, feeling uneasy. She was quiet and liked to keep her head down. But she knew if she let Agnes get away with her comments, the usual whispers would start up again about whether Margaret really belonged at school. She couldn't let that happen, couldn't let this new girl undermine her.

"I'm Caucasian, same as you," Margaret muttered. Agnes's eyes narrowed, but Margaret went on. Her voice getting louder, she said what her parents had told her to say if anyone questioned her place at the school. "My father is from India, yes, but not everyone in India is the same. My family is from northern India. We're Caucasian."

She didn't know why it mattered what part of India her father was from, or what a "Caucasian" even was, really.

Sometimes people said "Caucasian" when they meant "white." The word seemed to be a passport to the white world, the world Mother had been born into, the world where even if Margaret had to constantly justify herself, she was better off than most of Father's people, men who worked in the fields of the Central Valley.

"If you say so," Agnes said, seeming intimidated by Margaret's language but not entirely convinced.

"*I* say so," Bettina said fiercely. "And I say that if you bother Margaret anymore, you'll have to deal with me. And you'll find dirt in your lunch pail, and no one will feel sorry for you, because Margaret's been here longer than you have." She turned to Margaret. "I guess it wasn't worth getting to know her. Come, let's go sit over there."

As they walked away, Margaret whispered to Bettina, "Thanks. You know I don't like to get into fights."

"You stood up for yourself, though. That's good. You're too shy sometimes, you know. People like Agnes will walk all over you if you let them." They sat down under the shade of a cypress tree. Bettina pulled out a Karl May novel. The title was in German, so Margaret couldn't read it, but she could see from the cover that it was a Western.

Margaret wanted to tell her that she would stick out even more if she stood up for herself all the time. But Bettina had just come to her rescue. It didn't matter if she didn't completely understand; she was a good friend.

"Well, I didn't let her," Margaret said finally. "And neither did you."

~

It was harder than usual to get home that day—something big was going on in the city. Margaret did her best to avoid any large crowds, as her parents had told her to do after the Preparedness Day bombing the previous year. Ten people had been killed in an attack on a San Francisco parade.

With a sigh of relief, she turned onto her street and headed toward her family's storefront. The door to the store stood open, but there was no one at the counter. Margaret felt a tinge of unease.

Maybe her parents were upstairs, where her family lived on the second floor? As she walked over to the back staircase, she heard her parents' animated voices coming from the stockroom.

Should she try to listen? Or would that just make Father angry, since he had warned her against eavesdropping? Turning firmly away from temptation, she took the stairs two at a time. Yet even as she unlocked the door at the top, she wondered what they could be talking about.

Well, there was no point second-guessing her decision. She busied herself with clearing away the *San Francisco Chronicle* from the kitchen table so she could have a snack. But when she moved the newspaper, she found something more interesting than her parents' muffled conversation—a pamphlet about India! The title page read: *Exclusion of Hindus from America due to British Influence.*

Margaret began to read. The writer warned that the British government would not prevent a new American law against immigration from India from being passed, because it was too worried that the Hindus would "become imbued with pestiferous ideas of political freedom!"

She paused over the word "pestiferous." It was a funny-sounding word, and clearly the writer meant to be funny, for how could freedom ever be "pestiferous," whatever bad, pest-like thing that meant? She looked for the author's name on the cover. Ram Chandra, "editor of the *Hindustan Gadar*," was listed as the writer.

Gadar? That must be referring to the party her father had spoken of, the party of revolt. No wonder the author

mocked the British. The party must have put out this pamphlet, and that was why Father had it.

Absorbed by her discovery, she barely registered the door opening again as Father and Mother came up from the shop.

"What's that you're reading?" Father asked, and Margaret jumped a little. She showed him the cover. "Oh. That's an old one. I meant to throw it out, now that Ram Chandra's created so much trouble, but he does write well." He took back the pamphlet. "May as well keep it."

Mother entered the kitchen as well. "Ah, Margaret! Back from school. I suppose you've heard already."

Heard what? And why is no one downstairs watching the shop? Margaret tilted her head in curiosity.

"What the president said yesterday," Mother went on. "It's on the front page. I suppose there wasn't much of a choice, after the Germans sank our ships."

Now Margaret looked at the newspaper she'd pushed half off the table.

WAR WITH GERMANY, the headline blared.

No wonder it had been so hard to get home! No wonder her parents had left the shop. The country was going to war. The kaiser had finally gone too far, and now America would be joining the Allies, France and Russia and Great Britain . . .

"It's going to be bad," Mother was saying. "War fever is a terrible thing. It makes you not recognize your own neighbors anymore. I remember after the war with Spain . . . Well, we'd better hope it's over soon. And I can't say the kaiser wasn't asking for it."

Margaret barely paid attention, her mind swirling with thoughts. America wasn't a neutral country anymore. It was an ally of Britain and an enemy of Germany. Did that mean Father's friends, taking German money to end British rule, were now traitors to the United States? Did that mean they weren't safe? She tried to catch Father's eye and failed. He was avoiding her gaze.

"Don't you have a friend who's German?" Mother continued.

It took Margaret a moment to understand. She was so worried about Father, it hadn't even occurred to her to think of her best friend. "Bettina will be so upset," she finally said.

"Does she still have family there?" Mother asked.

Margaret nodded. "It's her father who came over. She still has aunts and uncles and cousins in Prussia."

Mother shook her head. "That's too bad. War is a terrible thing." She sighed as she headed back downstairs. "I'd better lock up the shop for the night."

Father finally met Margaret's eyes. When Mother's footsteps had died out, he said, "Don't worry. We'll be fine."

By *we*, he must have meant himself and his Ghadar Party friends. But why wait until Mother had gone to reassure her? "Mother doesn't know," Margaret guessed.

Father tensed. After a moment, he said, "She knows I give money to the Ghadar Party." He said it so carefully, though, that she knew exactly what he was doing. He was trying not to lie to her.

It was strange, Father dodging her words, like he was one of her schoolmates afraid she'd get him in trouble. He usually exuded a quiet confidence. Now he was hesitating and weighing his words like a guilty person.

"She doesn't know about the Germans," she pressed on, relentless.

"No," he admitted. "And keep your voice down. It's not good to talk about that now."

Should she tell Mother what was going on? No one liked tattletales, but this was important. Only there wasn't anything Mother could do about it.

"It would only make it more dangerous for her if she knew," Father said, as if he could read her thoughts. "We'll be fine," he repeated, and she wondered if he was trying to convince her or himself.

~

That night, Margaret practiced the Longfellow poem they were supposed to memorize for school. The words clip-clopped along like hoofbeats, and the subject was fascinating. Paul Revere had been a conspirator too, plotting with his friend for a secret signal as the British advanced. She read on, excitement coursing through her veins:

The fate of a nation was riding that night;

And the spark struck out by that steed, in his flight,
Kindled the land into flame with its heat.

She savored the words and the image of a country catching fire. But soon came the reminder of the risks Paul Revere and the other patriots had taken:

And one was safe and asleep in his bed
Who at the bridge would be first to fall,
Who that day would be lying dead,
Pierced by a British musket-ball.

A shudder ran through Margaret. She closed the book.

SAN FRANCISCO CHRONICLE

April 6, 1917

UNITED STATES DECLARES WAR ON GERMANY

The American government has declared war on Germany, provoked by the sinking of five American merchant ships in submarine attacks by German U-boats and attempts by the German foreign secretary to incite war between Mexico and the United States.

President Woodrow Wilson expressed his hope that American action would "make the world safe for democracy." America now joins Great Britain and France in fighting Germany and its allies, Austria-Hungary and the Ottoman Empire.

San Francisco marked the occasion with a military parade and the unfurling of a large flag.

Chapter 3

Spring 1917

"That'll be two seventy-five—no, wait, seventy-nine."

Margaret hated working the till in her parents' shop. Stocking the shelves was fine, even interesting when they had a shipment of spices. Greeting the customers and helping them find things was fun too. But she struggled with making change and totaling prices.

She hoped Father would be done with his meeting soon. A recent batch of vegetables had been infested with bugs. Father had gone into the back of the shop with the supplier, upset and threatening to cut off future contracts. Until that issue was resolved, she was stuck at the till. She envied Bettina, whose father taught German at university. Bettina never had to help with her father's work, only look after the little brother she often complained of.

Though would Bettina's father have much work now? Two days ago, war had been declared, and Margaret didn't think many people would want to learn German now. As had long been rumored, her own school had gotten rid of the class immediately.

Margaret's father and the supplier finally returned.

"Thank you for the second chance, Ranjit," the supplier said. "It won't happen again."

Margaret thought Father was too lenient for his own good sometimes, but she supposed that if he were a strict businessman, he would be a strict father too, and that would be awful.

Father waved the supplier out and took over the till. "Thank you," he said to her. "What a mess that was. At least the bugs don't seem to have spread. If he sends another batch like that—" He abruptly straightened. "How can I help you, Inspector?"

Two police officers had just come in. These weren't patrols off the street but polished officials. The columns of buttons down the fronts of their uniforms shone. One of them presented a detective's badge in the shape of the San Francisco Police Department's funny seven-pointed star.

Margaret sucked in a breath. There was only one reason detectives would be here, in her family's little produce store. Her fears had come true.

"Are you Ranjit Singh?" one of the men asked. Father nodded. "We have a warrant for your arrest. Please come with us."

With a shaky breath, Father said, "Margaret, lock up the store and go upstairs to your mother. I'm sure this is a mistake and I'll be right back."

Margaret nodded, but her feet were frozen in place. She was sure this was no mistake—they'd come to take Father away because of what he was mixed up in with the Ghadar Party. Maybe they'd even deport him. He'd said they were safe in a neutral country, but America wasn't a neutral country anymore.

"Margaret!"

She shook herself and took the keys Father held out to her.

"I'll be fine. Be good and listen to your mother." He looked her in the eye for a moment, then patted her on the head and followed the inspectors out.

A few customers were watching with baffled expressions. "What's going on here? What do those police want with him?" one customer asked.

Margaret took a deep breath. Parroting Father, she said, "I'm sure this is a mistake. I need to lock up the store. Please come back some other time."

The customers left, shooting glances over their shoulders as they did so. Margaret locked the door behind them and then raced upstairs to her family's apartment above the shop.

"Mother! Mother!"

Mother looked up from the stove, where she was stirring a big pot of soup. "What is it, dear? Shouldn't you be in the store helping your father?"

"They've taken him away, and I don't think they'll let him go . . . It's because of the kaiser . . . When we were in Stockton . . ." Margaret paused to catch her breath.

Mother dropped the wooden spoon, and hot soup splashed onto the wall. "What do you mean, 'taken him away'? Who's taken him away? Where is he?"

"The police!"

"'The police?'" Mother echoed. "What do you mean? Why would they do that? He's never done anything against the law."

The whole story spilled out: what Margaret had seen and heard at the gurdwara, including the suspicious man eavesdropping, and what Father had told her afterward.

Mother sat down on the stool by the stove with a thump. "I knew about the Ghadar Party—he always sent them a bit of money. 'For India's freedom,' he said. And I approved of it! Everyone should be free—I've always thought so. But I didn't know they were working with the kaiser. How many of our ships has Germany sunk with its U-boats just in the last few weeks? Oh, how could Ranjit have been so naive as to get involved with something like this?"

When she put it like that, Father's involvement did sound like a very bad idea. But Margaret felt like she should speak up for Father, who wasn't there to defend himself. "It's not as if they were doing anything against America. We weren't even in the war until the day before yesterday. Besides, aren't they just like the patriots in the Revolutionary War? Who worked with France and everything? We learned that in school."

Mother squinted at her. "Did your father tell you that's what they were—like the patriots?"

"He said America fought for freedom against Britain, and the Ghadar Party's no different."

A burst of laughter escaped Mother, though she didn't look very amused, and Margaret didn't know what she'd said that was so funny.

"Isn't it true?" Margaret asked.

"It's not wrong," Mother said. "It's the way you said it. You see, when you're young, you think everything is so clear-cut. Patriots and loyalists, Indians and the British, good people and bad people. I used to be like that too. But even good people do bad things sometimes. I just hope they'll let him go. Your father wouldn't hurt a fly."

Margaret thought he might, if it was a British fly. Father was a gentle man, but he'd also talked about using force and guns to make the British leave India.

"I hope they let him go soon." Margaret said.

Mother shook her head. "Hope won't be enough, though. I have to go call Mr. Cahill."

Father had always made sure to have a lawyer to consult, both before he married Mother—in case of any difficulties with an interracial marriage, which was very uncommon and in some places illegal—and when he moved to San Francisco and started his business. Mr. Cahill had come highly recommended, and he'd helped many Indians and other Asians get around the state of California's restrictions on Asians owning farmland.

As Mother headed downstairs to use the store telephone, Margaret paced upstairs, restless. Why hadn't she been more insistent when telling Father about the man spying on them at the gurdwara? What if that man had gotten him arrested? She knew there was probably nothing she could have done to stop it, but why hadn't she told Father to stop working with the Ghadar Party?

That was a funny thought, her telling Father not to do something. As if he, who'd crossed an ocean, would listen to a young girl who'd never so much as been outside California. Besides, she'd been so caught up in what he was telling her about India that she'd almost entirely agreed with him. Even now, despite Mother calling Father naive, Margaret wasn't sure what he'd done was wrong. Only dangerous.

All she was certain of was that she wanted Father to come home safely, and quickly.

Dear Mr. R. Singh,

I have never been more surprised in all my years as a lawyer than when I found out you had been arrested in yesterday's sweep. Yes, it was a sweep—more than one hundred people have been arrested, Hindu and American and German. I even heard of a Hindu student turning himself in because he wrongly believed all the Hindus in the state were being arrested. All because of this plot, and this Ghadar Party.

From what I understand, you're accused of violating the neutrality of the United States and forming a military enterprise —or, in less fancy legal terminology, you were plotting against Britain from the safety of America as part of the German war effort, which isn't something even a neutral country can allow. And of course, we're not neutral anymore.

I can't believe a family man like yourself would get mixed up with violent radicals like these Ghadar Party men. What would happen to your wife and daughter if you go to prison? You've told me how it hurts to see your country suffer under British rule and your countrymen disrespected. How would it feel to see your own family suffer, though?

I'm hopeful we can get you released—they're really

looking for the ringleaders, the students and the educated men. As far as they're concerned, you're just a shopkeeper who might have given the Ghadar Party some money and encouragement. And that's not as bad. But you'll have to keep your head down when you get out. Don't go and do anything reckless, because it's more than prison you have to fear. I'm worried that the government will deport some of the party members to India, where, as you know, the British won't look kindly on their efforts.

Believe me, I understand your feelings—my father was an Irishman, and I have family members in Ireland who were caught up in the uprising last year. America being allied with Britain isn't an easy thing to swallow. But let me tell you: the kaiser doesn't care a bit about India except as a way to hurt the British. And Germany's the enemy of America now. I don't think most people will understand why the Ghadar Party men worked with the Germans.

At any rate, I hope to get you out soon.

Best regards,
Peter Cahill
Attorney-at-Law, Cahill & Foster Ltd.

Chapter 4

Spring 1917

Margaret didn't go to school the next day. She was sure the news would have spread, and she couldn't face the idea of having to go through her normal routine while Father was in jail, of having all the other girls ask her questions, of hearing Agnes's gloating. Mr. Cahill said dozens of Hindus had been arrested, not just in San Francisco but all over the state. Mr. Cahill also said Father would soon be back. She didn't know if he meant it or was just saying that to make Mother and her feel better.

So she moped around the house and did chores with Mother, who barely noticed her and moved as if in a trance, dazed by the disaster.

They didn't open the store that day. Soon they would have to, whether or not Father came back. They would need the money. But Margaret thought Mother couldn't face their customers any more than Margaret could her peers. The only person from school whom she really missed was Bettina. Surely Bettina would have understood. They were best friends, and besides, Bettina's family was German. She wouldn't be angry that Father had worked with Germany. But even seeing Bettina wouldn't make going back to school worth it.

The next day, however, Margaret's mother had recovered enough to put her foot down. "I won't have you missing any more school. You know your father would want you to get an education. You're going whether you like it or not."

And that was that. No matter how queasy the thought of school made her, she had to go.

~

Bettina was waiting for Margaret by the door of the schoolhouse, probably wondering where she'd been the day before.

Margaret ran up to her friend and hugged her tightly. "I'm so glad to see you, Bettina!"

A couple girls elbowed past them, and she realized they were blocking the main entrance. She let go of Bettina and moved onto the lawn.

"You should call me Betty now," Bettina said, following her. "And what's wrong?"

"Betty?" Margaret wrinkled her nose. "Why? Bettina's so much nicer."

"Betty is a good American name," Bettina said, lifting her chin defiantly. "And I want everyone to know I'm an American, not a German. Now tell me what's wrong. Why weren't you here yesterday? Ugh, I had no one to practice that long Revere poem with, and I completely flubbed it when it was my turn to recite."

Margaret shifted uncomfortably. "You don't know what's happened?"

Bettina—no, *Betty*—looked blank. "Know what?"

She hadn't even heard about the arrests that had rocked Margaret's world. Margaret was trying to get up the nerve to tell her when the bell rang for class. They ran inside and took off down the hall.

"Know what, Margaret?" Betty called after her, but Margaret focused on making it to class on time. Out of breath, they slid into class at the last minute, almost knocking over their shared desk as they scrambled behind it. Any whispering died down as the teacher came in. Betty kept shooting her inquisitive looks, though.

Margaret couldn't focus on the equations Miss Taylor was explaining. Fractions were bad enough on an ordinary day, but now all she could think of was Father. Would he be out soon, as Mr. Cahill had said, or would he spend years in jail, not coming out until she was grown up? Did he have enough to eat? Was he even safe, what with all the criminals in jail—and the guards who would think him a traitor?

"Margaret Singh!"

Margaret jerked out of her anxious daze. The teacher and most of the class were staring at her. Betty's forehead was creased with concern. Miss Taylor just looked irritated.

"I'm sorry?" She had clearly missed something. It was hard to care.

"I said, can you reduce four-eighths for me?"

"I . . . it's . . . um . . ."

Betty tilted her slate toward Margaret.

"One-half!" Margaret read, too quickly.

Miss Taylor was not fooled. "No more daydreaming, Margaret. And Betty, keep your answers to yourself."

She wasn't daydreaming, though. More like living in a waking nightmare.

~

Halfway through the awkward hour that had recently been German class and was now French, the principal appeared in the doorway. Ordinarily, he was the sort of person who had to fight to look stern, but now he was grave and unsmiling.

"Can I borrow Margaret Singh?"

Betty shot Margaret another of those questioning looks. Margaret stood and walked out. It had to be about Father. Not paying attention in class wouldn't be enough to concern the principal.

The principal walked to his office in silence, and Margaret followed, hurrying to keep up with his long strides. He sat down behind his desk. Margaret stood in front, hands clasped.

"I've recently heard about your father's arrest," he said, without any lead-up. "Now, I don't judge any of my students by their parents' actions or origins. I only expect that while they're in school, they behave themselves and show loyalty to this country. I don't know what you've been hearing at home, but here you must show yourself to be a good American, whatever your father has done and whatever Hindu notions he has."

Her face burned. It was easy for him to say she should show loyalty. But nodding along with his words felt like disloyalty to Father and his "Hindu notions." She tried saying nothing, and an awkward silence fell over the office.

"Margaret?"

She thought, *If I don't say anything, he'll think I don't mean to be a good American. I stick out enough already; I have to fit in. Father will understand that I have to keep my head down.*

"Yes, sir," she said, looking at the floor.

The principal relaxed. "Now, I didn't have you come here just to tell you that. Your mother telephoned to say your father's been released and she wants you to come home right away."

Margaret almost bounced off the floor. Father was free! A big grin spread across her face, and the principal smiled, looking more like his usual jovial self.

"You're excused for the remainder of the day. But now that this is sorted out, I hope you won't be missing any more school." He nodded toward the door.

"Thank you!" She almost ran out of the office, and once in the hallway, she did run—and didn't bother stopping at the classroom to pick up her slate and her lunch pail. Father was back!

She tore through the streets to her stop, heedless of motorcars and carts and passersby. On the streetcar, she couldn't sit still. It felt like forever before she got home.

The store was locked, but she headed up the back entrance to the second floor. As she unlocked the door to their home, she saw her parents standing in the kitchen, a little apart from each other. Their voices drowned out the sound of the lock clicking. They appeared to be arguing.

She'd expected a joyful reunion. What could they be fighting about?

Margaret remembered Father's warning against eavesdropping. But just a little couldn't hurt, could it? She hovered on the threshold.

"You didn't tell me any of this!" Mother's high-pitched voice rose even further. "You didn't say this group you were involved with was running guns or taking German money or anything! I had to find out from my own daughter after you were arrested!"

"Margaret only found out by accident," Father said, defending himself. "I never meant to drag her into this."

"And when did you mean to drag *me* into it? When did you mean to tell me what was really going on? I'm your wife, don't I have a right to know?" The pain in Mother's voice was obvious.

"I knew you'd be upset, so I didn't . . ." Father spread his hands as if to say, *What could I do?*

"I might have been upset, true, but I'm more upset now," Mother said, more quietly now. "I've learned I can't trust you to tell me the truth. And about something this important too. Something I should have known about *before* police came to take you away."

Still standing on the threshold, Margaret winced. She didn't see her parents fight often, and watching them quarrel now hurt. How many times would she have to hear something she didn't want to before she would learn not to listen in? She wanted to stop their arguing, but what could she do? Maybe if she went inside and they noticed her, they'd stop. They almost never quarreled in front of her.

She walked in and, putting on a cheery voice, called out, "Father! You're home!"

Her parents froze. She saw Mother force a smile and Father's creased forehead smooth out as they, too, tried to pretend nothing had happened.

Father snatched her up in an embrace. Mother smiled as she watched them. Burying her face in Father's chest, Margaret could almost believe the past two days had just been a bad dream. Her father was safe. That was the only important thing.

"Rani," Father said. It was one of the few Punjabi words she knew, meaning "queen." Father sometimes

called her that as a pet name. "It's all right. I'm not going anywhere."

~

Margaret barely let Father out of her sight all through the rest of the morning and afternoon. It wasn't difficult, as he barely moved from the secondhand armchair that was the most comfortable seat they had. The whole ordeal might seem a mere nightmare now, but Margaret could see the traces of it on her father's face. He had dark shadows under his eyes, and though he tried to put on a smile for her, he was clearly exhausted.

Mother stayed in the kitchen, cooking an especially fine lunch, she said, but Margaret suspected she wanted to stay out of the way after the argument. The meal itself, though tasty, felt strange; they ate in near silence. She could feel the strain between her parents, even though they did not quarrel again.

The last forty-eight hours had wrung Margaret out. She needed to talk to someone about all of it and to escape the unexpected tension. So when she knew school was out for the day, she headed over to see Bettina. *Betty*, she reminded herself, *Betty*.

She knocked on the door of Betty's fancy house. It was a new house, built after the earthquake—like most of the buildings in the city—and it was solid and spacious. Margaret had been a bit scared the first time she'd gone to visit her friend and found out she lived in so nice a place, with a full-time maid and all, while Margaret's family lived in a few rooms over the shop. That fear had more or less disappeared over the years, especially since Betty's professor father had turned out to be less disappointed that his daughter had befriended the half-Indian daughter of a small-time shopkeeper than that Margaret and her father didn't know even a little bit of Sanskrit, the ancient Indian tongue in which epics were written. Betty's mother was still a little sniffy about Margaret, though.

The door opened, and the maid, who was only a few years older than Margaret and Betty, called out, "Miss Bettina, your friend is here."

Betty came running. "What's going on? Why did the principal pull you out of class? Why were you acting so strange this morning?" She grabbed Margaret's hand and pulled her in. "Come on upstairs. Tell me everything!"

They bounded up the stairs to Betty's room. Familiar piles of books in English and German tilted precariously on the bedside table and the bureau. Thick, leather-bound volumes of German classics like the Brothers Grimm, Goethe, and E.T.A. Hoffmann lay side by side with cheap copies of Jack London's *The Sea-Wolf*, Jules Verne's *The Golden Volcano*, and what seemed like an infinite number of those Karl May novels. Betty had always preferred adventure stories to the serious literature her father made sure she read.

Betty now flopped down on the bed, while Margaret closed the door and sat in the desk chair.

"My father was arrested," she said baldly. Betty gasped, and Margaret hurried to reassure her. "Don't worry, he's back home now."

"But what was he arrested for? Did he do something illegal?"

After making Betty promise not to tell anyone, Margaret started to explain, but Betty kept interrupting with questions. "What's the Ghadar Party? Why do the Hindus need Germany? Why didn't you tell me any of this before? Is your father a spy?"

"Of course not!" Margaret snapped after that last question. "He just wants his country to be free! America wasn't even in the war when this started."

That didn't seem to satisfy her friend.

"What does your father say about the kaiser?" Betty asked, looking grave.

"I don't remember, and what does it matter? Why do you care? You're German anyway."

Betty recoiled, her face crumpling before she said angrily, "Just because my father was born in Germany doesn't mean I'm not American. And we're at war with Germany now. You should be careful what you say."

"What do you mean?" Margaret wasn't sure what she'd said wrong, but she knew she'd hurt Betty's feelings. "I'm sorry, I didn't mean to say anything rude."

"I'm an American, and so are you. Only the two of us will have to prove it, and if you keep saying foolish things, people will notice."

"What do you mean?" Margaret repeated.

"Don't you realize there's a war going on? What do you think people will say when they find out your father was arrested for plotting with Germany? They'll say you're disloyal, or worse!"

"We'll be fine if we keep our heads down," Margaret said, surprised by Betty's vehemence. "It can't be that bad." At least, it couldn't be much worse than normal. So many people already thought she barely belonged, if at all.

"Keeping your head down isn't enough anymore. Not in wartime," Betty said solemnly, as if repeating something she'd been told. Then her voice changed, becoming almost menacing. "Don't tell anyone else what your father was arrested for."

Frightened now, Margaret nodded. First her parents had fought, and now Betty was acting strangely as well. *You won't recognize your own neighbors*, Mother had said when the war was declared. But Margaret hadn't expected changes to come to the people closest to her. It frightened her almost as much as Father's arrest.

The ground was shifting under her, like an earthquake. Hopefully it would pass as quickly as one, but she knew how much damage earthquakes left in their wake.

SAN FRANCISCO TIMES

April 10, 1917

HINDUS, GERMANS, AND AMERICANS CHARGED IN CONSPIRACY

Nine Germans, nine Americans, and seventeen Hindus will be tried in San Francisco later this year for violating US neutrality laws. This is part of a larger effort to bring to justice those involved in a massive plot against the United Kingdom. Their plans included smuggling weapons on the ship *Annie Larsen* and working with German agents and Irish republicans. One of the agents involved was the top German diplomat in San Francisco. Now that the international conspiracy has been discovered, the Hindus face the possibility of being deported to India if they are found guilty, where they could face the death penalty.

Chapter 5

Spring 1917

Early Saturday morning, Margaret stood under the "Fletcher and Singh's Greengrocer" sign, watching her parents arrange crates of tomatoes. Fletcher was Mother's maiden name. Her parents had thought that putting it on the sign would lessen the obvious foreignness of Father's surname, while the Sikh name Singh signaled that spices and other ingredients of Indian cooking could be bought there.

"This trial will be a bad thing for us," Father was saying. "We'll have to be careful."

"Well," Mother said, laughing a bit, "it isn't our first brush with the law."

Mother and Father had gotten over their differences quickly, and Margaret was very glad that her parents weren't fighting anymore. But she didn't know what Mother was talking about.

"What do you mean, 'not your first brush'?" she asked.

Her parents looked at her with surprise.

"Aren't you supposed to be minding the till?" Father asked.

"There aren't any customers yet. I just came outside for a bit of fresh air."

"Well, then, you can help out here. Not the peaches, that crate is too heavy for you. I don't want them spilling—they bruise. How about you put up the baskets of berries?"

Margaret started arranging the baskets of blackberries and strawberries, but she refused to be put off. "What was your first brush with the law, Mother?"

"Oh, I was a bit of a firebrand in my youth," Mother said with a false smile. "You wouldn't believe the trouble I would get into." Her voice was overly light and airy.

"What do you mean?" Margaret repeated. "Did you break the law?"

Mother looked uncomfortable. "It was all a long time ago. Trying to organize coal miners and such, after the big explosion back when I lived in Bellingham. I wasn't very good at organizing. And a lot of the unions hate Asians, as I found out when I got married."

It was hard to imagine her mother, a quiet housewife, as some sort of radical, even if it had been long ago. But then, it was also hard to picture her father being involved in a conspiracy.

"Your mother," Father said, "has always stood up for her beliefs, whatever the cost. She married me even though she lost her citizenship because of it."

"What?" Margaret gaped.

"Don't say 'what' like that, Margaret. It's not polite," Mother chided her.

Margaret shook her head. The mismatch between Mother's current self, a stickler for etiquette, and the past Margaret was just learning about confused her. "But why did you have to give up your citizenship? I didn't know that!"

"Any woman who marries a foreigner has to. A woman's citizenship follows that of her husband. Jeannette Rankin is trying to change that in Congress, but she probably won't get anywhere. She's the only woman, and the men don't care; they don't lose their citizenship if they marry a foreigner."

"But that's so unfair!"

Mother laughed. "Do you think I don't know that? Even though women have the vote in California, I can't vote because I'm no longer counted as an American, and if I travel abroad, I might not be let back in the country. But if it's the price I have to pay to have my family, I'm happy to pay it." She smiled up at Father.

Margaret mulled this over, watching them. She thought about her mother among the coal miners of Washington State, where she used to live. Her parents always said Bellingham was beautiful, between the mountains and the ocean, but she'd never seen it.

"Why do we never go back to Bellingham?" she asked abruptly. "Don't we have friends there?"

Mother ducked into the store. "I'll just be at the counter in case anyone comes in." There was a strain in her voice that wasn't there before, and Margaret wondered if she'd upset her mother by reminding her of the past. Maybe she didn't want to go back to Bellingham ever again—or maybe she couldn't.

"You know your mother doesn't get along with her parents," Father said softly, once Mother was gone.

Margaret had never met her Fletcher grandparents, and she'd always accepted this as the reason why. Now, though, she was starting to wonder.

"It isn't because of any trouble with the law or anything?" she asked. Were her parents fugitives from justice? It seemed less ridiculous an idea after Father's arrest.

Father smiled. "No, of course not. Actually, Washington State is one of the only places that doesn't have a law against any kind of intermarriage."

She hadn't been thinking of that—she'd been wondering about the past her mother had hinted at earlier.

"Not that they didn't *try* to get the law on us," Father added, bending over a crate of lettuce.

Something crashed into place in Margaret's mind. "My grandparents? Is that who you mean?"

Father froze, seeming to realize he'd given away too much. Then he straightened and said, "I suppose you're old enough to know by now. Yes, your grandparents weren't very happy about us. They called the police on me when they found out we'd run away and gotten married."

Margaret's eyes widened. "What happened then?"

"Well, the police arrested me, of course. Then they realized there wasn't any law against what we'd done, so they said they were keeping me for my own protection. After a day, they had to let me go. And you were on the way, by then. Your grandparents had to accept our marriage. They gave your mother some money to leave Bellingham so they wouldn't have to live with the shame of a Sikh son-in-law. They were not sorry to see her go. We came to San Francisco and used the money to set up our store. We were lucky, really."

It was Father's constant refrain, but Margaret didn't think it fit here, in this story of hostile relatives and wrongful arrest. "I don't see how. You had to leave everything you knew."

Father was silent as he lifted the crate of lettuce. Margaret grabbed one side, trying to help.

He ruffled her hair when they had finally moved it into place. "Thank you. It wasn't so bad, you know. I'd already left everything familiar behind once, leaving my family in Punjab. I'd only been in Bellingham a few years, and it wasn't home to me. Your mother suffered more. She'd been there her whole life. But at least we got out before the riots."

"What riots?"

"Only a little bit later, there was rioting in Bellingham. The Asiatic Exclusion League started attacking and beating the Indians who worked in the lumber mills—the same mills where I'd been working. So of course the police arrested the Indians—for their own protection, they said. Most of the Indians in Bellingham left for Canada or other parts after that. Which is why I don't have any particular friends there."

Margaret said indignantly, "But the Asiatic Exclusion League is here in San Francisco too. How are they allowed, after they caused a riot?"

Father's brow furrowed. "It's not that simple. The League has many labor unions and politicians supporting it. And frankly, most whites think the Asiatic Exclusion League has a point. Look at how black people are treated. White Americans say all men are created equal, and that's true, but they don't act like it. Many people don't want us here."

The last crate stacked in place, Father turned to go inside. Margaret followed slowly, lost in thought. No wonder Mother didn't like to talk about her parents. They were like Agnes, wrinkling her nose at the thought of having to share her school with an Asian, except even worse. They had to be, if they'd called the police on Father.

And to think, all this time, she hadn't known anything of what had happened back in Bellingham. What else didn't she know about her parents' lives?

~

Spreckels Lake was one of Margaret's favorite places in the city. She and Betty met up by the artificial lake when they could to dangle their feet in the water and watch the model boats float by.

The sky was clear, and the sunlight glinted off the water and the iridescent green feathers of the mallard ducks. But despite the beauty of the afternoon, Betty didn't seem to be enjoying herself. Margaret's usually outgoing friend was quiet and preoccupied.

"Is your family all right? In Germany?" Margaret asked.

"Hush," Betty said. "They're fine. I don't want to talk about it." She kicked her feet in the lake, splashing Margaret's. "How's your father?"

"He's fine, just worried. Some of the people he knows are going on trial."

"People from his country?"

"And some Germans, and some Irish too. Let's not talk about it."

"Right," Betty agreed. There was an awkward silence for a moment. Margaret tried to figure out what they could talk about instead.

"Let's see if we can spot a turtle," she finally said. "I saw one last time I was here."

They did not succeed. Betty thought she'd found one, but it turned out to be a slime-covered rock. There were other distractions on the lake, though, including a splendid heron spreading its wings as it fished for food. Margaret and Betty cooed over a group of ducklings following their mother, and a tiny model yacht came almost near enough for them to touch.

"That Agnes has been asking questions about you. She was bothering me when we were both rolling bandages at Junior Red Cross," Betty said. "She wants to know why the principal pulled you out of class and how you got into the school in the first place."

Margaret tensed up. "You didn't tell her anything, did you?" She was glad she hadn't gone to volunteer with Betty, if Agnes was going to be causing trouble there.

"Of course not! I'm your friend, and she has it out for me too now."

"She's such a little . . ." Margaret stopped herself from using a bad word. "Such a . . ." But she couldn't think of anything else to call Agnes.

Betty laughed. "She's awful, I know. But no one will listen to her. We all know you belong."

That was comforting, but not exactly true. The other girls at school weren't so obvious about it as Agnes, but Margaret sensed they felt uneasy having her in their class.

"Come on, let's go walk in the park," said Margaret, drying her feet off and putting her stockings and shoes back on.

Betty followed. "The park is where my family lived after the big earthquake," she said. "Mutti—Mother, I mean—told me we lived in a tent here for months. She said the whole park was covered in tents. It was like after a war or something."

Margaret wondered again about Betty's family in Germany. Were they really fine, as she'd said, despite the war? "Is your family really all right?"

Betty stared. "That was eleven years ago."

"No, I mean your aunts and uncles and grandparents."

"I told you not to ask about that anymore! They're in Berlin, far away from the fighting." Betty paused. Then her fierce look softened to something sadder. "Which is good, because with the mail being how it is, I don't think we'll hear from them again for a long while."

Margaret wondered what exactly she meant, but Betty had made it clear the conversation was over, so she didn't say anything. They wandered in the leafy shade for a bit, enjoying the mild afternoon. But there wasn't much to talk about.

Finally Betty said, "I should be getting home."

Margaret nodded. The outing had been strangely unsatisfying.

September 15, 1917

We've been back at school for a while now so I figured I should get back to writing. In some ways, school is the same as usual—math class is still awful. French is nice, though, and I chose to keep studying it this year even though the school now has a Spanish teacher as well. Betty doesn't have such a great advantage over me anymore, as she had to start from the beginning in French too. She doesn't seem to mind the change, not as much as I would have. We're so competitive about French that we're both near the top of the class!

Our teacher is a Belgian, Mme. Lambert. Another girl told me Mme. Lambert's brother was shot by the German army. He wasn't even a soldier, but they took him hostage and killed him.

Everyone is so tense lately, on the lookout for anything that's not patriotic. The teachers have gotten a lot stricter about good English—we're not supposed to say "Yep" or "Yah" for "Yes," especially since "Yah" sounds like the German "Ja." All over the city there are posters to "Buy Liberty Bonds," which will help fund the war effort. They have scary pictures of German soldiers on them, saying the Huns will win if we don't fight back, or things like, "Are you 100 percent American? Prove it!"

Whenever I see that poster, it makes me think of Betty and how she's so obviously 100 percent American, volunteering all the time to support the war effort. I also think of my father, who can probably never become American. Even before he was arrested, it would have been hard, because only white or African immigrants can become American citizens, and no one's entirely sure whether anyone from India might possibly count as white. Most of the time, we don't. I barely got into the white school in the first place. I know they only let me in as a favor to my mother, because she bothered the principal so much about it.

Am I 100 percent American? I've never lived in any other country, so how could I be anything else? I'm an American citizen, even though Mother and Father aren't. And I love living in California. I wouldn't know what to do in India. But when people say 100 percent American these days, they mean people who look 100 percent like themselves.

Chapter 6

Autumn 1917

This year, Margaret and her family were not late to the gurdwara. They went to Stockton for the full three days of Guru Nanak Gurpurab, at Father's insistence. Margaret guessed he wanted to see his friends, especially after all the trouble with the arrests and the upcoming trial.

The first two days of the festival were taken up with a nonstop reading of the Guru Granth Sahib, the holy book. Margaret didn't understand a word of it because it was not translated. Father told her that even he didn't understand every word, since it drew from a number of different languages. Fortunately, there was plenty of food available, and the readers took turns so that no one had to read aloud for the full forty-eight hours.

When they weren't listening to the recitation, the men talked in Punjabi. Everyone was a little on edge this year, and a few loud arguments broke out outside the gurdwara. Many of the men wore traditional knives, or kirpans, but Margaret wasn't worried—the knives, her father had explained long ago, were only used for protecting the innocent and as a symbol of the faith. They weren't for use in ordinary quarrels.

Father didn't wear one, though. When she asked him why not, he replied cryptically. "For the same reason I don't wear a turban."

"And why is that?"

"I used to, before I married your mother. It's how I was raised, and I had to in my army days—it's in the regulations. But I cut my long hair when I got married and took off my turban and my kirpan." He sighed. "I didn't want us to stick out so much. Besides, I wasn't as religious as I used to be back in India. I used to travel to the Golden Temple and think about the great teachers of my religion. I still believe in one God, but I'm not sure anymore exactly what He wants."

Margaret thought about that. Certainly it was hard to know what God wanted. It was hard enough to know what the *people* around her wanted sometimes, and she could talk to them. She understood his other reason better, though. Standing out in a crowd wasn't easy.

"Then why did we come here for three whole days?" she asked.

Father laughed. "Are you so very bored? There's nowhere else I can see all my friends and learn the latest news. Muslims and Hindus come here to the temple for that too, not just Sikhs. It's nice to be around people who are like us."

The third day of the festival was much more fun. They sang hymns—well, most people sang, while Margaret mouthed along because she didn't know the words. People also carried the holy book around on a beautifully decorated palanquin. It was a very different experience from the Christian church they went to in San Francisco on holidays to honor her mother's faith, where there were many copies of the Bible—here the whole congregation had only the one copy of the Guru Granth Sahib, and it was revered.

Then came Margaret's favorite part—langar. She ate the meal so fast she got the hiccups and had to excuse herself, taking a quick walk in the fresh air to calm them. Pausing to lean against the railing of one of the gurdwara's big staircases, she remembered last year, listening in on Father's conversation and seeing the other eavesdropper. She still didn't know if he'd had anything to do with Father's arrest or if she had been imagining things. She hadn't imagined the rest of it, though.

At least Father was safe. He wasn't being charged with the leaders of the Ghadar Party in the trial going forward in San Francisco. It didn't sound like the party had been very successful overall. The major uprisings they'd planned in India hadn't caught on.

She hiccupped again, just when she'd thought her hiccups were gone. The noise startled a man sitting at the bottom of the stairs. No, not a man—a boy. He was a few years older than her, and he wore a turban. It wasn't as big as most of the men's, probably because his hair hadn't grown very long yet.

Her parents had always told her not to talk to strange men, but did that necessarily include strange boys?

It probably did. She knew Father wouldn't approve. But she might have met a boy his age at her school, in the upper grades. Though she wouldn't meet another Punjabi there. And she never really had a chance to talk to the young men at the gurdwara—they were always catching up with each other in groups, talking in Punjabi and not especially interested in spending time with her. Now curiosity got the better of her.

The boy was sitting alone. There couldn't be anything wrong with going over and introducing herself. Feeling a little daring, she headed down the stairs, another hiccup escaping as she approached.

"I bet they heard that all the way inside," the boy said, smiling. "You're Ranjit's daughter?"

Margaret was used to people at the gurdwara knowing who she was even though she didn't know them.

"I'm Gurdeep," he said before she could ask. "What're you doing out here by yourself?"

She didn't like his tone, as if he were so much older than her and she only a young child. "Same as you," she said, trying to look at ease.

He laughed. "I bet that's not true. I came outside to do this," he said, waving a toothpick that he'd been using to clean his teeth. "Now tell me, little girl—"

"I'm not a little girl. I'm only a bit younger than you are!" she snapped. "Just because you're a boy doesn't make you so grown-up!" A hiccup jolted her, spoiling the effect of her words. Blushing, she turned to go back inside. What had she been thinking? Just because he was younger than most people around here didn't mean he'd want to talk to her as an equal.

"Wait. I'm sorry," Gurdeep called out. "Come back, I didn't mean to be rude."

She turned around. "What do you want?"

"Just to talk. You don't see a lot of girls around here," he went on. "I'll stop picking my teeth if you want."

She started down the stairs cautiously. "I don't mind," she said, even though she found it disgusting to watch. She sat down a few steps above him. "Just don't call me 'little girl.' I have a name. It's Margaret."

"Margaret," he repeated. "That's such an American name. Your mother's American?"

She nodded.

"Are you in school, or working?"

"In school."

"I've been working in the fields since I was your age, you know. When I came over, I was the youngest Indian on the ship. The immigration officials barely let me in, but I came in through San Francisco, where the inspector's a bit more lenient than in some other ports. I wanted to go to Canada, but it's hard to get in these days, even though it's also part of the British Empire. Anyway, I went through Angel Island."

"The immigration officials don't let women and children into America, right? My father told me."

"No. The men had to leave their wives and children behind. I wonder if you've got an older brother or sister back in India."

Margaret had never thought of that. She knew people married much younger in India, but Father didn't speak much about his family, only sometimes mentioning he had a brother. Now she wondered if she had a sibling there. Nieces and nephews. What if Father had a wife still waiting for him? The idea bothered her.

"I don't think my father would have done that," she said. "He loves my mother. I'm sure he'd never be a bigamist." She didn't know why she was discussing Father's private business with a stranger, except she felt the need to defend him.

Gurdeep smiled. "It's different there. You marry a person because your parents and their parents think it would be a good idea. They arrange the whole thing between them. It's not a love match like your parents have. How did that come about? Americans hate it when a white woman marries someone like us."

Here she was on firmer ground. "My parents ran away together when they were living in Washington State. It was a scandal in their town, and the police were even called."

"By your grandparents, I'd guess?"

"I've never met them. In the end, they gave my parents some money if they'd go away and settle somewhere else."

Gurdeep whistled. "That's quite a story. A real romance."

"They're lucky they left. They were living near Bellingham, where the riots happened."

Gurdeep winced and said, "I wasn't here then, but I've heard about it. Sometimes I wonder what was the point of coming to America at all, if they hate us so much."

He dug in particularly hard with the toothpick, straining to get something out. Margaret tried not to stare, but she couldn't help it. He said such strange things. There was hatred in this country—her parents had seen plenty of it—but there was also opportunity. And she'd never lived anywhere else.

"I'm glad to live here," she said. "It's my home. And besides, isn't it better than having to live under the British?"

Popping the toothpick out of his mouth and laughing, he said, "Your father must have told you that." Then he grew serious. "There are fewer of us here, though. And the government doesn't want us here at all—there's a new law against any more laborers coming from Asia. The Barred Zone, they call it."

Margaret didn't like the sound of that. She shook her head. "There's nothing we can do about it. Besides, you're already here. They won't send you back."

Gurdeep frowned. "It's still not right, though. Back home, they think America is a country of freedom and justice. A republic with equality for all. But then we got here and found out that was only for the whites. It's all a lot of hypocrisy." He kicked out against the stairs as he said it.

"It's not so bad as all that," Margaret said softly. "Not all the time, anyway." *Not for me*, she meant.

Gurdeep picked up on what she hadn't said aloud. "Easy for you to say. Your mother is white, and you're not a laborer. I suppose you go to a white school?"

"I didn't mean it that way." Margaret blushed. She struggled for something to say. "I just think . . . maybe this isn't such a bad thing, this Barred Zone. Maybe the government will stop worrying so much about us once there aren't any more Indians coming in."

"So you want to pull up the ladder behind you? It was all right for your father to come, but no more immigrants now so you can fit in?" Gurdeep made a noise of disgust, throwing down his toothpick. "I think not. We have to stand up for ourselves. That's the only way anyone will respect us."

His eyes burned, and Margaret was swept up by his words, just as she had been by Father's the previous year. But then she thought about how few they were and how the Ghadar Party's whole plan for freeing India had been easily rolled up by the law. Besides, working with the kaiser certainly hadn't made anyone respect them.

"How?" she asked. "How do we stand up for ourselves?"

Gurdeep was about to answer, but at that moment, a shadow fell over Margaret.

"Margaret, what are you doing here?" Father's voice shook with unaccustomed anger. "I've been looking all over for you, and I find you talking to a strange boy alone!"

"Ranjit, I meant no harm," Gurdeep said in English. Then he switched to Punjabi, but Margaret's father ignored him.

"Haven't I taught you better than that?" Father yelled at Margaret.

Tears stung her eyes. She wasn't used to Father being angry with her. He was normally such an easygoing person, even when he was upset. She knew she had made a mistake, but Gurdeep had seemed harmless enough.

Father grabbed her arm, and they went back upstairs. Before they reentered the gurdwara, Father said in a low voice, "Stay near your mother or me from now on. I don't want to catch you wandering off again."

"But Father, I just wanted to talk to someone my own age," she protested.

"It's our last day here—you can listen to me for that long. You never know what could happen when you go off alone with a boy you don't know."

Margaret held her tongue, but she didn't think anything bad would have happened to her. Gurdeep didn't seem dangerous, just lonely. And he'd given her plenty to think about. What if she were going about her life the wrong way, trying to keep her head down because she was already different enough? What if that wouldn't actually help her or anyone else? Maybe Gurdeep was right, and standing firm was the only way to win respect.

Chapter 7

Autumn 1917

Father's anger had blown over by the time they boarded the train for San Francisco. He thanked Mother and her for coming to Stockton for longer than usual, and he was clearly cheered up by having seen his friends. It occurred to Margaret that he must be a bit lonely—she had her schoolmates, and Mother had a few friends from various societies around town, but most of the time, Father had the store and them, and that was it. And, though he didn't wear a turban, there was no way he could hide his skin color and accent.

Still thinking about what Gurdeep had told her, she asked him on the train, "Father, do you ever wish you hadn't come here?"

He startled. "What? Not have you and your mother? Why would I ever wish such a thing?"

"I don't know," Margaret said. "I was just wondering. I thought maybe you missed home." She couldn't say, *Because that boy I was talking to said something that made me think.* But she added, "And because of how no one wants us here."

Father tilted his head and looked at her intently. His forehead furrowed in concern. "Margaret, has something happened at school?"

"No, I'm fine," she said hurriedly.

Father took a hardboiled egg out from their bundle of snacks and cracked its shell against his knee. Peeling it, he said, "I barely got here in the first place. The immigration officers turn away more than half of the Indians who try to come. They say Asians will become a public charge, that we'll be poor and make trouble for the government because we can't find work. But there's plenty of work to be had. Do you know the reason they say we won't find it? Because Americans won't want to hire us! But I was lucky. I've always been lucky. Here, have an egg."

He passed the bundle to Mother and Margaret. The train jolted as he did so, and the hardboiled eggs rolled away onto the floor. Margaret scrambled to grab them from under the seat, and when she emerged, the conversation had drifted on. Father and Mother were talking about store business.

Margaret sat in silence. She had never questioned that Father was a lucky man—after all, he said so constantly. Though he joked about his countrymen's fondness for astrology, he often referred to his good luck, saying he was lucky to have a wife and child here where there weren't many Indian women, lucky to have escaped the Bellingham riots, lucky to have been released so soon after his arrest, lucky to have gotten into the United States at all.

But now she thought that most men had a wife and children. Most Europeans who tried to enter the United States could. If Father had been a white man, his "luck" would have seemed quite ordinary.

What if, instead, he was an unlucky man? But luck in this case wasn't written in the stars. Her father's bad luck was, she reflected as California whizzed past the train window, very definitely man-made.

~

Fall passed into winter, and Christmas came with its pageants and sleigh bells. Mother took Margaret to the church they went to on big holidays, and Father, as usual, came too, though he wasn't a Christian. Betty's family went to a different church, a Lutheran one, but they invited Margaret to their annual sumptuous Christmas dinner. Even Betty's snobbish mother couldn't spoil the feast. It was spectacular, with a roast goose, mulled wine, and a special bread with dried fruit and nuts called stollen. This bounty came despite the fact that Betty's father had less work this year. Few students at his university wanted to learn German, because of the war.

The changes brought by the war kept coming. At school, Margaret heard of other students' older brothers being drafted into the army. Betty, like many of their classmates, had thrown herself into volunteering with the Junior Red Cross, rolling bandages for hospitals for wounded soldiers and sending friendship boxes to children in war-torn Europe. Margaret went with her one evening and helped make splints. It could have been fun, on its own—getting to know some of her other classmates outside of school, learning more about nursing and how hospitals worked—but as part of the barrage of posters and slogans that the war had brought, it just felt like a dreary obligation. There was something stifling about the pressure to volunteer, to show how loyal you were.

Change had come to the world outside school as well. Part of Stanford University's land had been turned into a military training area, Camp Fremont. The Presidio, the old army fortress that had been around since California was a part of Mexico, continued to expand. Troops trained to fight in Europe, and officers trained to lead them.

Not all the news was about the war, though. Just before Christmas, someone bombed the California Governor's Mansion. All the newspapers were pretty sure it was members of the radical labor union, the Industrial Workers of the World. Luckily, the governor had not been hurt. Margaret's parents were not particularly fond of him—he was no friend of Asian immigrants—but her mother was still grateful he had escaped injury.

"I'm glad he wasn't killed," Mother said. "Can you imagine how much worse things would have gotten?

How much more suspicious everyone would be of their neighbors?"

Father disagreed. "I'm not going to rejoice in his survival." His normally gentle voice was steely, and suddenly Margaret understood how he could have been a soldier once—and how he could have come to decide that guns and bombs would be needed to drive out the British.

It was a pretty dismal way to end 1917. Margaret hoped the new year would bring better circumstances. But things only kept getting more and more uncomfortable. She felt like she was swallowing her feelings most of the time, not that she knew exactly how to articulate them. All she knew was that she was suffocating.

~

Miss Taylor paused during her lecture about the Declaration of Independence. "Who can tell me about the similarities between our Declaration and England's Magna Carta?"

Margaret could think of a couple of answers, but she didn't raise her hand. Miss Taylor looked expectantly at her but moved on when she saw Margaret wasn't volunteering this time. It wasn't easy to get answers out of the students, some of whom had probably forgotten what the Magna Carta was. History was usually Margaret's favorite class—and where she shined above her bored classmates. She loved hearing the thrilling stories of the past and making connections between events. But the war had changed history class too. Nowadays, even lessons on the war between Britain and America had to show how the two countries were really natural allies.

Margaret wasn't surprised when Miss Taylor brought the discussion back to the war. "It's the history and institutions, from trial by jury to habeas corpus to democracy itself, that we have in common. These have led us to become allies in the war for democracy against the imperialist powers. And speaking of the war, our next discussion will be on saving sugar, Meatless Mondays, and other thrifty measures you and your families can take to help our boys at the front. But first, lunch!"

The bell rang, and the usual rush to the door began. Margaret and Betty hung back until the first stampede was over. It meant not getting the best spots at lunch, but it also helped them avoid being elbowed or shoved in the hurry to get out of class first.

It was too chilly to eat outside, they agreed, and so Betty and Margaret sat down on the edges of a long table in the lunchroom. As it was Monday, not even the richest of her classmates had any meat. Betty stared sadly at her portion of barley soup. Margaret didn't mind. The vegetarian meal reminded her of langar at the gurdwara, though it certainly wasn't as spicy.

Thinking of the Sikh festival made her think of Gurdeep. And the history lesson was still bothering her. Was just quietly refusing to raise her hand going to change anything?

Betty waved her hand in front of Margaret's face. "Are you all right? You seem . . . distracted."

"I'm fine," Margaret said quickly. "Just thinking."

Then she took a deep breath, like she was about to jump off a rock at the beach. Betty probably wouldn't like what she was going to say, but she felt the need to say it anyway. "I'm just so tired of hearing Miss Taylor always say what a great ally Britain is, and how much the British love freedom and democracy."

Betty frowned but didn't say anything for a while. Then she asked, head cocked to one side, "Why?"

"Because of what they do in India."

Betty still looked quizzical. She gestured for Margaret to go on. Margaret started to tell Betty what Father had told her about what life was like in India under British rule. As she spoke, more and more of the other students turned to listen to her. She felt a little thrill as she spoke to the whole table.

"Don't you remember how before the war started, we heard more about how America stood up to Britain during the revolution and how we had to fight to get self-rule here? What's the difference between that and what Indian revolutionaries are trying to do now? Don't they deserve freedom too?"

Betty nodded, but from the other end of the table, Agnes called out, "India wouldn't get anywhere without Britain. Everyone knows that. It's not like America was—it's poor and backward."

Margaret's hands curled into fists under the table. "That's not true—"

"Besides," Agnes went on, "it's mostly just Germans and Indians stirring up trouble, like the ones who are on trial now. Secret agents. Wasn't your father arrested too?"

Margaret could feel the shift as the whole table looked at Agnes, waiting for her to say more.

"It's the truth," Agnes said, curling a lock of her auburn hair around her finger. "Remember that day she was pulled out of class last year? I asked around, and her father was in jail! He was part of the conspiracy. That's why she's talking down about our allies. Her own family's working with the Germans."

Annie, a girl Margaret had gotten to know better at the Junior Red Cross, stood up with a scowl. "Oh, can it, Agnes. You've always had it in for Margaret. You've been waiting all year for the chance to let this little tidbit drop. Just because she's picked up some strange ideas doesn't make her a traitor." Annie grabbed her things and left. Margaret wished she'd stayed, because the rest of the table was deathly still.

"Is it true, Margaret?" her classmate Minnie asked in a small voice.

Margaret looked around helplessly. She couldn't make herself say anything. She flashed a pleading glance at Betty, who had cowed Agnes before. But Betty was silent and staring at the table.

"It's true," Agnes said. "She can't deny it. And she's always sitting and whispering with that Bettina Schmidt, whose Hun family's probably killing Americans right now."

Betty reddened. "I'm no traitor. You leave me alone."

"You were eating up every word Margaret said earlier."

Betty looked from Agnes to Margaret and back again. "I was not. Not even a little."

Margaret gaped. "You're the one who asked me about it!"

Betty said, "Look, Margaret, you're my friend, but you say foolish things sometimes. Watch what you say, or you'll get into trouble." She stood up and flounced off.

~

The rest of the day was awful. Betty traded desks when they got back to class, and Margaret found herself sitting next to Minnie, who kept shooting her strange looks, and Laura, whose brother was at war in France and who wouldn't so much as let Margaret borrow a bit of chalk when hers broke. Even Annie didn't seem much inclined to defend her any further.

But all of that paled next to Betty's behavior. Margaret just couldn't believe how Betty was treating her. They'd been friends for years. They'd always done everything together. Yes, Betty had acted strangely when she'd first heard of Margaret's father's arrest, but that had been almost a year ago. They'd just been celebrating Christmas together a few weeks ago! She could have dealt with all the other girls hating her if only Betty had stood up for her.

When French class let out and everyone started to go home, Margaret hung back. As she grabbed her coat to go out, it got caught on the hook, and a long tear ripped down the lining. She tried to untangle it but only managed to tear the fabric further. This was the last thing she needed today. Furious, she kicked the wall and wrenched her coat off the hook. She didn't care how much she damaged it. She flung it over her shoulder and strode away, knocking over one of the desks.

"What are you doing? Pick that back up!" A hand fell on Margaret's shoulders and turned her around. "Look at me when I—what's wrong?" Mme. Lambert's voice softened as she saw Margaret's face. "Margaret, are you unwell?"

Margaret shook her head. "No, Madame."

"You don't look well. What's the matter?"

Her teacher looked so gentle and concerned that Margaret was tempted to tell the truth. But how could she tell Mme. Lambert that the others thought her a traitor? Mme. Lambert, who was from occupied Belgium, who'd lost her own brother to the kaiser's army. She swallowed down the words. "Nothing, Madame."

"Are you quite sure?" When she nodded, Mme. Lambert sighed, as if she knew Margaret was lying. "Well, then. Pick up the desk you knocked over, and make sure you get some rest when you go home."

Her classmates thought she was a traitor. All of them, even Betty. They probably thought she'd picked up "Hindu notions," as the principal had said, or "pestiferous ideas," as the pamphlet had called it. But was the idea that everyone had the right to freedom so strange? President Wilson himself had just said in his message to the world, his Fourteen Points, that every country should choose its own institutions. How was what she had said so different?

January 10, 1918

I've never been so miserable. I'm used to Agnes being horrible, but this is different. Betty won't talk to me. Neither will almost anyone else. If this is what comes of standing up for myself, then Gurdeep was wrong. It's not worth it. I feel so stupid now. But I won't say sorry for what I did. I didn't do anything wrong.

Mother asked me why I'm so quiet these days, but I didn't tell her. Would she even understand? Maybe. Father said she was always one to stand up for her beliefs, but she at least always had a choice about sticking out in the first place.

Father's busy with the store and hasn't noticed anything's wrong. I'm glad, because it's mostly his fault. If he hadn't been arrested, none of this would have happened. I wish it hadn't. Sometimes I want to tell him so.

But he would feel so bad if he knew, and it's hard to be angry with him. He was only doing what was best for his homeland. Now, thanks to him, I feel like a stranger in mine.

Father doesn't seem very hopeful these days. I asked him about the Fourteen Points and if they meant India would be free at the end of the war. He said some people think that, but while President Wilson says nice things, he probably only means to give freedom to European nations. Father said he used to think India could appeal to the president's ideal of self-determination (I asked what that meant, and it means that every nation has a right to choose its own course freely). But now Father doesn't have much time for Wilson.

And the trial is still going on. They say it will be one of the biggest and most expensive ever in American history.

Chapter 8

Spring 1918

Margaret had had enough.

The uproar had faded a bit in the week since Agnes told everyone about Father's arrest and declared that Margaret was disloyal. People weren't shunning her completely anymore. She could borrow a pen nib if she needed it. But she had no one to sit with at lunch and no one to talk to after class. She was alone.

And she was furious. She stewed on how Betty had abandoned her when she needed her most, until she was angrier than she was sad or frightened. Hadn't it been Betty herself who'd often said Margaret was too quiet, too willing to let people like Agnes walk all over her? But then when Margaret spoke up, Betty acted as if she had nothing to do with her, as if it was just Margaret "saying foolish things." What was the matter with her?

All week, Betty had managed to avoid her. Well, today that wouldn't work. Margaret would confront her and see what she had to say for herself.

She didn't do it at lunch, where everyone would be able to hear them. Instead, she waited until after school let out. She stood a little ways away from the school building. A few of her classmates passed by, but they ignored her, and she them.

As she waited, she realized the flaws in her plan. What if Betty was with a group? She could just ignore Margaret. What if—and this one hurt to admit—Betty was alone but still wouldn't talk to her?

If she won't talk to me even alone, I'll go away, Margaret thought. *I'm not going to beg for her friendship*. But it was easy to think and harder to do. Who else did she have at school?

Finally, she spotted Betty's messy blond curls. Her former best friend was staring straight ahead, an almost angry look on her face. She didn't seem to notice Margaret at all.

As she passed, Margaret called out to her. "Betty! I need to talk to you!"

Betty didn't stop.

"You can't just keep ignoring me! Betty!"

Betty turned, then looked over her shoulder to check that no one else was around. She whispered harshly, "What do you want?"

Margaret considered for a moment. What she wanted was for everything to go back to normal. But "normal" meant trying to fit in, biting her tongue, and not saying anything that could upset her fragile position. "Normal" meant being afraid. A line came to her from the Longfellow poem they had memorized last year, just before her father's arrest: "A cry of defiance, and not of fear." The clip-clop hoofbeats of the poem's rhythm pounded like her heart in her chest.

"I want to know why you've been ignoring me," she said.

Betty stared at her for a moment, then barked out a laugh. "You don't understand at all, do you?"

"I understand that you've been treating me like dirt. First you encouraged me to say what I thought, and then the moment I did, you abandoned me!"

Betty looked from side to side, checking again that they weren't observed. "Let's not talk here. I can't be seen with you. Come over to my house later today, around five." Then she hurried off down the street, her curly hair escaping its pins as the wind blew through it.

Margaret watched her go. That had gone better than it could have, but now she wondered what Betty was going to tell her later. What explanation could she possibly give? Would this be the end of their friendship?

~

Just before five, Margaret caught the streetcar toward Betty's house. The car was crowded, so she had to stand most of the way as they rattled up and down the hills of San Francisco. But it wasn't the sudden stops and starts that gave Margaret the ache in her stomach.

It wasn't far from the nearest stop to Betty's house, but Margaret dragged the walk out. Then she stood on the doorstep for a while, working up the courage to ring the bell. An old man next door, whom she hadn't seen before, gave her a funny look as he puttered about his yard.

Now or never, she thought. She rang the doorbell.

Betty answered. She beckoned for Margaret to follow. They crept through the house to avoid disturbing Betty's father, and for a moment, it felt like old times as they shared a conspiratorial look. But then Betty's grin disappeared. They made their way to Betty's bedroom, where Margaret still had to pick her way among piles of books, most of them in English now.

Betty shut the door behind them. "I know you're mad at me," she began, "but you don't know how hard it's been."

This wasn't what Margaret had been expecting. Not at all. "I thought *you* were mad at *me*!"

"I was," Betty said, collapsing into her desk chair with a thump. "I was so angry, at first. Because you didn't seem to understand. It was like you were trying to drag me down with you, when you told Agnes that I'd been the one who'd got you talking in the first place, when you wouldn't let me—"

Margaret's voice shook with anger. "Wouldn't let you what? Pretend you had nothing to do with me?"

"You don't know what it's been like this whole year!" Betty yelled. Then she lowered her voice. "You've been so off in your own world ever since your father was arrested, you didn't even notice what it was like for me. How hard I've had to fight to fit in. It's not so easy anymore, having a last name like Schmidt."

Margaret didn't know what to say. Betty, fighting for acceptance? Sure, she'd heard what Agnes had said about Betty's "Hun family," but Betty was always so American, so patriotic. Surely everyone saw that. Or was that why Betty was always so insistent on her patriotism, right down to changing her name? Because she knew other people would question it?

"But why didn't you just tell me why you were upset?" Margaret asked. "Why cut me off like that?"

"Because I was scared," Betty said quietly. "Scared what the others would think of me, if I kept being friends with you. That they'd think I was a traitor."

That didn't seem like Betty. Not the girl who'd threatened Agnes in Margaret's defense last year and told Margaret she shouldn't let people walk all over her.

"You always told me to stand up for myself," Margaret said, puzzled.

"I know. But I didn't really understand what it was like, having everyone question whether you belong. And you acted like I should understand what your father did, just because my family's originally from Germany. It's not just people like Agnes who assume I'm disloyal somehow. You do it too, even though you don't mean any harm. You don't even know why my family left Europe."

It was true. Margaret had never asked. She'd just assumed it was the same story as most people's: poverty there and opportunity here. "Why did they leave, then?"

"My mother's family came here after 1848 as refugees when the revolutions failed. My father left because there was a warrant for his arrest. A political case. That was under the old emperor, but still." Betty laughed wryly. "We have more reason to hate the kaiser and all his kin than most Americans do."

Then she grew serious again. "It's so unfair that after all that, we're called traitors and Huns by people who don't know anything about us. As if all Germans are the same. My family tried to make Germany a better place and had to leave because of it."

"You're right," Margaret said, taking it all in. "I had no idea." Why had she never wondered?

"It didn't seem to matter so much, before," Betty admitted.

"It's always mattered, for me," Margaret said. "All my life, people have been acting as if I didn't belong, or if I did, it was only on certain conditions. I'm sick of it. I've tried keeping my head down. I've tried speaking up. Nothing works." She sighed. "I'm so tired."

"You must hate me right now," Betty said. "For turning my back on you."

"A little bit," Margaret admitted.

"But I had to, don't you see?"

"You always used to be so brave! Much braver than me." She'd always relied on Betty to confront bullies and gossip. Now she wondered whether that was fair.

Staring at the floor, Betty said, "No one can be brave all the time." She looked up. "I should have been brave enough to keep being your friend, though."

"You still can be. If you want."

Betty smiled. "I would like that."

~

Margaret smiled all the way back home. She and Betty were friends again! And now she understood why Betty had been acting so strangely. Betty had been fighting her own battle for over a year, one where Margaret had been a hindrance rather than a help. She could see, looking back over the assumptions she'd made about Betty since the war began, how much she'd been mistaken.

But they had overcome her mistakes and Betty's fears. And even though it wouldn't change how the other girls viewed her, Margaret knew she could face those difficulties now that she had her best friend back.

She bounced up the stairs and past Mother, who said, "You're a ray of sunshine all of a sudden. What's changed?"

Margaret instinctively tried to hide her feelings, remembering that she'd told her mother nothing of what had happened at school. "Oh, nothing. Just went over to Betty's house."

Mother frowned. "You ought to have more than just one friend, you know. I'm sure Betty's lovely, but there are other girls in your class, aren't there?"

Margaret had the funny feeling of standing outside herself, watching herself choose what to do. Her first thought was to say something neutral. The old her would have done that. The old her had spent a lot of time not saying things.

Now she said, "I don't have a lot of classmates willing to get close to someone like me."

The words hung in the air, heavy, impossible to take back. Someone like her? She didn't know anyone like her. She moved between the world of her parents, adults who'd carved out a place of their own, and the world of her school, where talking about things close to her heart had made even her best friend question her for a time.

No wonder Gurdeep's words had been a breath of fresh air. Their lives were distant—he was a farmworker and an immigrant—but he'd been the closest she'd gotten to someone like her. And he'd given her a choice where before there had only been one option. He'd given her permission to be honest about how she felt, rather than blending in at all costs.

"Things have changed a lot. With the trial, and everything. And with me."

Mother sat down at the kitchen table. "Tell me about it."

For the second time that day, Margaret was flooded with relief. Navigating these two worlds where no one was quite like her wasn't always going to be easy. It was probably never going to be easy. But she wasn't as alone as she'd thought.

Chapter 9

Spring 1918

It had been a little more than a year since war had been declared. Margaret and Betty were at the Junior Red Cross again, rolling bandages. At first, Margaret had resented Betty's insistence that they spend their evenings volunteering. But Margaret was coming to see the importance of their work as the older volunteers told stories about how the organization helped refugees and sent ships full of nurses, doctors, and supplies to Europe. The stories from the front were horrible: soldiers sick from breathing in poison gas and orphaned children in need of care.

Margaret understood now why her father always said he was lucky. Her standing at school had never recovered from her speaking out, and she and Betty were unpopular.

JUNIOR RED CRO

But so many would have traded places with them in a heartbeat. The war might be a messy intrusion into their lives, but at least they weren't living in its path, and they could do something for those who were.

But there were times when the old resentment flared up.

"The president of the United States himself is going to lead the Red Cross parade in New York City next month. We're going to have our own parade on May Day here, and the Juniors are going to get to march!" their supervisor told them proudly.

Margaret was glad that Woodrow Wilson wouldn't be at the San Francisco parade. She'd gotten her hopes up about the Fourteen Points, before Father told her what they really meant. Father had been so disappointed by the president and his talk—*only* talk—of freedom for all.

It was a relief to leave volunteering that evening. But Margaret wasn't the only one hurrying toward her home. There was the lawyer, Mr. Cahill, looking upset and with his hat on backward. Margaret couldn't help but panic.

"Mr. Cahill! What's the matter? Father isn't going to be arrested again, is he?" she asked as they almost bumped into each other at the entrance to the shop.

"No, no," he said, distracted. Then he caught sight of Father. "You won't believe what happened at the trial, Ranjit!" Mr. Cahill rushed in without even taking off his hat.

"What happened? They're not going to be deported, are they?" Margaret's mother called, walking over from the back room.

"I don't know, but that's not the point. Ram Singh shot someone! In court!"

At Margaret's and Mother's blank looks, Father explained, "Ram Singh was one of the Ghadar Party men on trial. What do you mean, he shot someone? Who did he shoot?"

"He shot one of his own men! Chandra something. Shot him dead right where he stood. I saw it with my own two eyes. Then the federal marshal guarding the court shot Ram Singh. He died then and there. So I guess we'll never know why he did it now."

"Wait a minute. It was Ram Chandra he shot?" Father asked. "That makes more sense now. Some in the party thought Ram Chandra was a British agent."

Margaret remembered the pamphlet with Ram Chandra's name on it, and that funny word, "pestiferous." Father had said he was planning to get rid of the booklet because of the author causing trouble. But could the man who wrote those fiery words really have been working for the British? It didn't make sense to her. And to think he had just been shot dead!

"I don't know the exact details," Mr. Cahill said. "You would know a lot more than I do, in this case."

"I'd definitely heard of serious problems between him and the others. Last year, he was ousted as editor of the Ghadar Party's paper. He set up a rival paper under the same name. Around then, we started to hear funny things about him. I'm not sure whether they were true. If he really betrayed us, I won't mourn him. But it's a bit of a shock. I'll ask around. Thank you for bringing the news."

"No trouble, it was on my way. By the by, they've convicted the Ghadar Party men, but no one got more than two years in prison. They probably won't be deported either, though I can't say for sure. I almost forgot about that in all the chaos." Mr. Cahill turned to go but then looked back. "You're a lucky man, Ranjit Singh."

"I know," Father said.

When Mr. Cahill had left, Father retreated upstairs to his bedroom, leaving Margaret and Mother to close the shop. When they went up to the kitchen, Margaret kept looking worriedly at the bedroom door.

"Don't fret," Mother said when she had glanced there for the umpteenth time. "He just needs to be alone right now. He didn't expect this."

Margaret wasn't sure whether her mother meant Ram Chandra's possible betrayal or Ram Singh's shocking actions.

Mother's gaze grew distant. "When there are only a few of you, and everyone's against you, you start getting paranoid. You start seeing enemies who aren't there, or magnifying small arguments into deadly ones. And you're already outside the law, so it seems a small step . . ." She shook her head. "I was quite radical as a young woman. As you can probably guess, I didn't quite fit in with my family or my hometown. But it turned out I wasn't cut out for radicalism either. And then came your father, and you. It didn't matter that we were despised—I'd finally found my home. Where I belonged."

Margaret smiled, a warm feeling coming over her. "With us?"

"Yes. Of course. Now help me get dinner started."

~

Father came out as they were just setting the table.

"That smells delicious," he said, as if everything were normal and he hadn't disappeared for hours.

They ate. Margaret and Mother filled the silence as best they could, but there wasn't much to say, and soon they stopped trying.

Father spoke at last. "It's only really just sunk in that I can't go back. To India. I wasn't going to, not after I got married here, but . . . the British and the Americans have been working hand in glove on this case. I could be arrested again if I went back there."

Margaret thought about never being able to come back to San Francisco, but she couldn't imagine it. Maybe because she'd never left California, never been apart from her family. Father had come all the way across an ocean, leaving everything familiar behind. But perhaps he'd always hoped to go back, if only just to visit or spend his old age there.

"I used to think I was just coming here for a while," Father went on. "Make some money and then go home. Things didn't work out that way, and I'm glad they didn't. But . . ." His voice faded.

Mother tried to cheer him up. "In all probability, they'll forget about it. Especially once the war ends. I can't imagine they're going to arrest everyone who supported the party—that would be most of the East Indians in America!"

"Probably I'm just being paranoid," Father said. "But I truly hope the government here doesn't deport those people. Several of our men have been executed in Lahore already. I don't like their chances if they're sent back."

Margaret remembered the first night she'd learned about the conspiracy, the fear she'd felt learning that a young student had been executed. The contrast with the light sentences the American court had handed down was dramatic. America might constantly dangle the promise of belonging in front of her only to snatch it away, but it was better to be here than there.

Still, she was curious about what she'd find if she went to India. What would it be like to see the glories of the Golden Temple in Amritsar, the holy site Father had traveled to as a young man? More importantly, what would it be like to go to his village and find her family? Did she have brothers and sisters there whom she'd never met, as Gurdeep had suggested? Did she have grandparents who might welcome her, unlike her grandparents in Washington State?

Or would that land, so far away and so unknown to her, be just another place where she didn't belong?

Someday, she promised herself, she'd take the steamship and see what her father's country was like. But she'd come back. Home wasn't necessarily where people looked like you. It could also be friends and family, as her mother had learned. And the people Margaret loved were right here.

April 24, 1918

Last night, I was so caught up in the book I was reading that I didn't notice everyone else had gone to sleep. Father eventually saw the light under my door when he got up in the night, and he scolded me for staying up late and leaving the lamp on to read "The Golden Mountain or some trash like that." (It's actually *The Golden Volcano*. I borrowed it from Betty. And it isn't trash. But that isn't the point.)

I apologized, and he left so I could wash up and change for bed. But when I opened my door again, Father didn't look well. Not angry or anything, but sad. I could guess why before he said anything. He was still thinking about the trial, and the news Mr. Cahill had brought.

Father asked me whether I was angry with him for everything that had happened since he was arrested. He said Mother told him that I was having trouble with my classmates because of it and that I should have told him about that.

"Everyone has to make sacrifices for freedom," he said, "but I see now why people drop away from the struggle when they get married and have children. Taking risks myself is one thing, but when it affects you and your mother . . ." He trailed off.

I didn't like to see him downhearted and doubting himself, but after all, wouldn't it have been easier for all of us if none of this had happened? If I'd never overheard him at the gurdwara, if he'd never been arrested? Life would have been much simpler for me. I would never have fought with Betty or argued with my classmates. I couldn't help but think Father was right. The Ghadar Party hadn't sparked mutiny and freed India, as they'd planned, after all. Nothing had changed.

But did that mean they were wrong to try? If no one ever tries to make things right, then things will stay wrong and unfair forever. Besides, I've learned so much this past year. I can't imagine going back.

So I told him, "It wasn't a mistake. you had to do something. Just because it didn't work doesn't mean it was wrong."

He smiled a little and thanked me before saying good night and closing the door.

It's morning now, and I have to get ready for school. But I wanted to write this down so I have it to return to later. That no matter all the trouble the last year and a half has brought, I wouldn't go back if I could.

Author's Note

In the early 1900s, thousands of men left British-ruled India for America in search of a better life. They ranged from farmers from the state of Punjab to students from all over India. Many came to California, where they worked on farms or studied at universities. They experienced discrimination, as many white Americans wanted to stop all immigration from Asia. Asian immigrants such as the Chinese, Japanese, Koreans, and Indians were not allowed to become US citizens. Chinese students were forced to attend segregated schools, while an agreement between the United States and Japan allowed Japanese students to attend white public schools. Racist organizations like the Asiatic Exclusion League advocated for stricter laws and sometimes resorted to violence, as in the Bellingham riots, when a mob attacked Indian lumber workers.

Still, Indians put down roots in America, with Sikhs establishing the first gurdwara in the country in Stockton, California. Many of the men married Mexican American women in the 1910s and later, creating mixed-race families. The first children of these marriages would have been very young at the time this novel is set. Earlier mixed marriages were rare, but they did occur—there are records of marriages between Indian men and white women, as in this book, and between Indian men and black women. Whether any of these marriages would have led to a child of Margaret's age growing up in San Francisco in the 1910s is a matter of speculation, and ultimately, Margaret and her family are fictional, though much of the book is based on real events.

The arrest of the Ghadar Party members in California really happened, and the trial that followed was known as the Hindu-German Conspiracy Trial. The Ghadar Party advocated for the violent overthrow of British colonial rule and the creation of an independent India. It was mainly supported by Indian immigrants who had experienced racism in their new country. The party was not able to gain widespread support inside India, where most groups at the time still advocated for greater rights within the British Empire rather than complete independence.

The Ghadar Party planned to take advantage of World War I to start a revolt among Indian soldiers in the British

Indian Army. To do this, they worked with Germany, Britain's main enemy in World War I. One of the Indians on trial really did shoot another in the courtroom before being shot himself. All eight were convicted, but they were not deported to India, as the British demanded, because there was public sympathy for their desire to free their country from British rule. Thus, they managed to escape execution, unlike the less fortunate Kartar Singh Sarabha, who returned from California to India and whose fate I described in the beginning of the book.

After the conspiracy failed, the Ghadar Party largely faded from the scene, despite smaller-scale attempts to resurrect it. Other groups and movements continued the effort to gain India's independence from Britain. They varied in the level of violence they used to achieve their goals, but through their diverse efforts, India won its independence in 1947.

During World War I, a surge of patriotism in the United States led to a fear of anyone considered "different." The state of California banned the teaching of German in public schools, and German Americans faced intense pressure to prove their loyalty. The Sedition Act of 1918 made it more difficult for people to criticize the US government without getting into legal trouble. Schools were encouraged to develop a sense of patriotism and support for the war effort in their students. Propaganda emphasized what the United States had in common with the United Kingdom and France, its allies in World War I, and what made Germany and other enemy countries different.

President Woodrow Wilson's Fourteen Points and emphasis on self-determination raised the hopes of people in countries oppressed by European colonialism, but those hopes were largely disappointed after the end of the war. Though some European countries, such as Poland, regained their independence right after the war, many non-European countries, such as India, had to wait until decades later.

My family came to the United States long after these events, but my father was born in India to a Punjabi family. His mother, my grandmother, is Sikh. Like Margaret, I am mixed-race; my mother is Italian. I was brought up learning about both American history and the Indian independence movement. Little did I know that the Indian independence movement was part of American history too.

To write this book, I relied largely on Seema Sohi's book *Echoes of Mutiny*, about the Ghadar Party in the United States, and the South Asian American Digital Archive, which makes important documents related to Indian American history available on the internet. Other sources included Nayan Shah's *Stranger Intimacy*, which explores the relationships—including interracial marriages—of early Asian immigrants on the West Coast, and Karen Leonard's *Making Ethnic Choices*, a study of the Punjabi Mexican community, which, while it focuses on a slightly later generation, provided important background information. The website of the Stockton gurdwara, which still serves as a place of worship today, was also a useful source.

Posters encouraged patriotism and reminded Americans of how to serve their country during World War I.

More than 1 million Indian soldiers fought for Britain during World War I, even as some Indian citizens struggled for India's independence.

World War I officially ended on November 11, 1918, when Germany signed an armistice with the Allies. Americans celebrated the war's end in Philadelphia, Pennsylvania.

Timeline

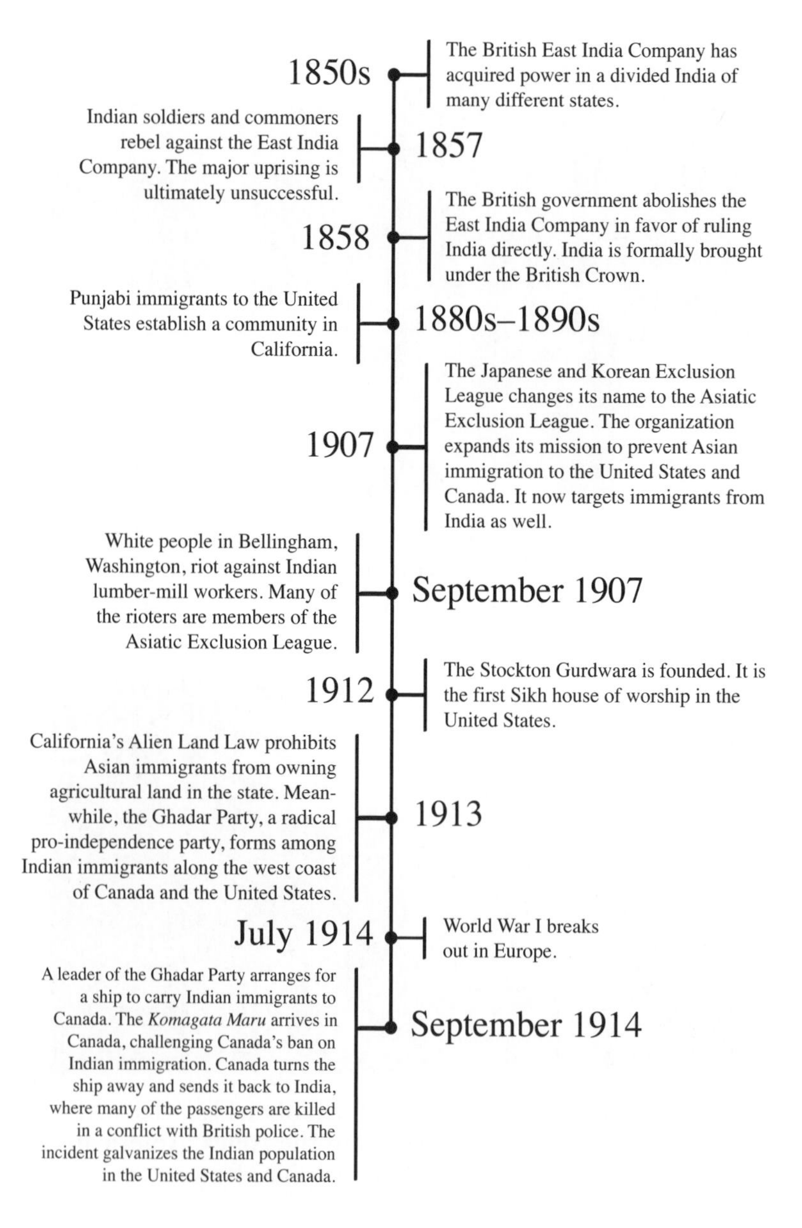
1850s
The British East India Company has acquired power in a divided India of many different states.
1857
Indian soldiers and commoners rebel against the East India Company. The major uprising is ultimately unsuccessful.
1858
The British government abolishes the East India Company in favor of ruling India directly. India is formally brought under the British Crown.
1880s–1890s
Punjabi immigrants to the United States establish a community in California.
1907
The Japanese and Korean Exclusion League changes its name to the Asiatic Exclusion League. The organization expands its mission to prevent Asian immigration to the United States and Canada. It now targets immigrants from India as well.
September 1907
White people in Bellingham, Washington, riot against Indian lumber-mill workers. Many of the rioters are members of the Asiatic Exclusion League.
1912
The Stockton Gurdwara is founded. It is the first Sikh house of worship in the United States.
1913
California's Alien Land Law prohibits Asian immigrants from owning agricultural land in the state. Meanwhile, the Ghadar Party, a radical pro-independence party, forms among Indian immigrants along the west coast of Canada and the United States.
July 1914
World War I breaks out in Europe.
September 1914
A leader of the Ghadar Party arranges for a ship to carry Indian immigrants to Canada. The *Komagata Maru* arrives in Canada, challenging Canada's ban on Indian immigration. Canada turns the ship away and sends it back to India, where many of the passengers are killed in a conflict with British police. The incident galvanizes the Indian population in the United States and Canada.

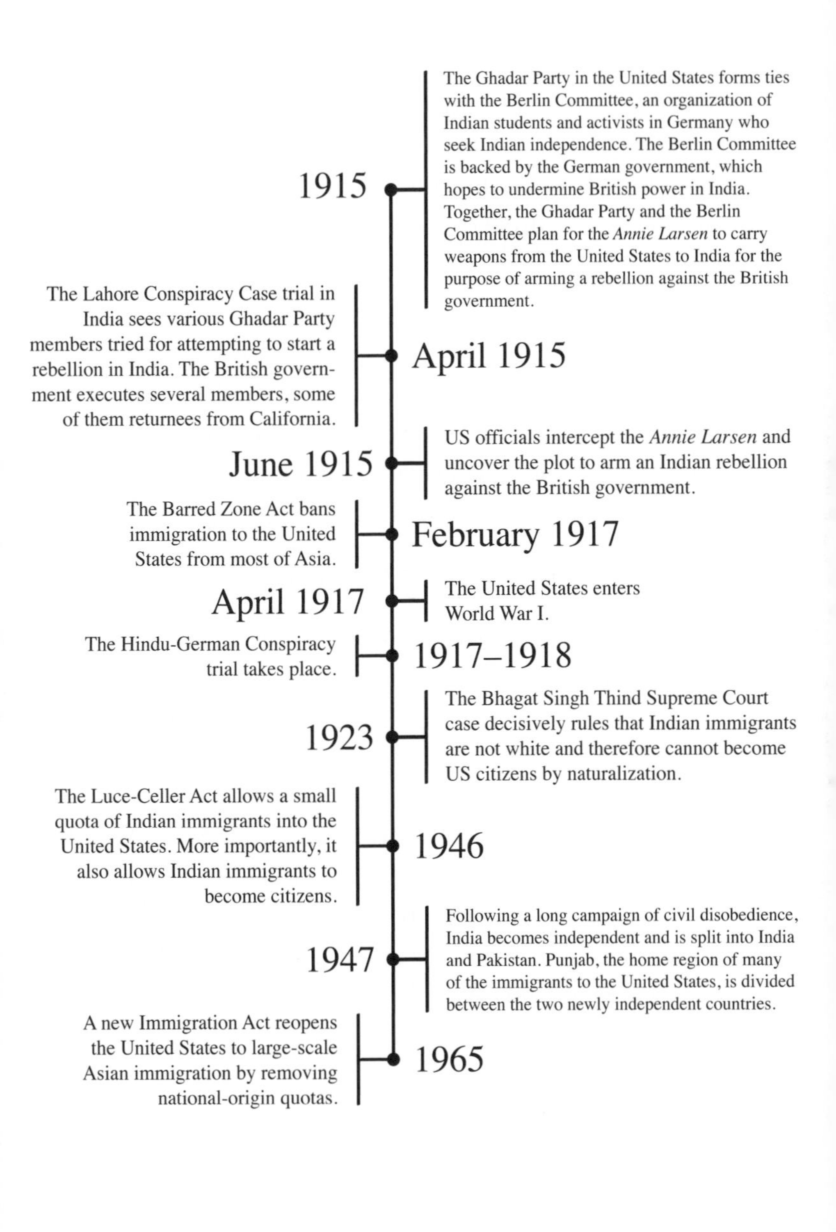
1915
The Ghadar Party in the United States forms ties with the Berlin Committee, an organization of Indian students and activists in Germany who seek Indian independence. The Berlin Committee is backed by the German government, which hopes to undermine British power in India. Together, the Ghadar Party and the Berlin Committee plan for the *Annie Larsen* to carry weapons from the United States to India for the purpose of arming a rebellion against the British government.
April 1915
The Lahore Conspiracy Case trial in India sees various Ghadar Party members tried for attempting to start a rebellion in India. The British government executes several members, some of them returnees from California.
June 1915
US officials intercept the *Annie Larsen* and uncover the plot to arm an Indian rebellion against the British government.
February 1917
The Barred Zone Act bans immigration to the United States from most of Asia.
April 1917
The United States enters World War I.
1917–1918
The Hindu-German Conspiracy trial takes place.
1923
The Bhagat Singh Thind Supreme Court case decisively rules that Indian immigrants are not white and therefore cannot become US citizens by naturalization.
1946
The Luce-Celler Act allows a small quota of Indian immigrants into the United States. More importantly, it also allows Indian immigrants to become citizens.
1947
Following a long campaign of civil disobedience, India becomes independent and is split into India and Pakistan. Punjab, the home region of many of the immigrants to the United States, is divided between the two newly independent countries.
1965
A new Immigration Act reopens the United States to large-scale Asian immigration by removing national-origin quotas.

About the Author

Maya Chhabra graduated from Georgetown University in 2015. Her short story for young adults, "Breaking," was published by *Cast of Wonders*. She also writes poetry and fiction for adults and translates from Russian. Born to Indian and Italian immigrant parents, she lives in Brooklyn with her partner.

About the Consultant

Rajan Gill is a professor of history at Yuba College. His work focuses on early twentieth-century Punjabi-Sikh immigration to the United States, the Ghadar Party, and immigrant identity.

About the Illustrator

Eric Freeberg has illustrated over twenty-five books for children, and has created work for magazines and ad campaigns. He was a winner of the 2010 London Book Fair's Children's Illustration Competition; the 2010 Holbein Prize for Fantasy Art, International Illustration Competition, Japan Illustrators' Association; Runner-Up, 2013 SCBWI Magazine Merit Award; Honorable Mention, 2009 SCBWI Don Freeman Portfolio Competition; and 2nd Prize, 2009 Clymer Museum's Annual Illustration Invitational. He was also a winner of the Elizabeth Greenshields Foundation Award.

PRAISE FOR

I Am America

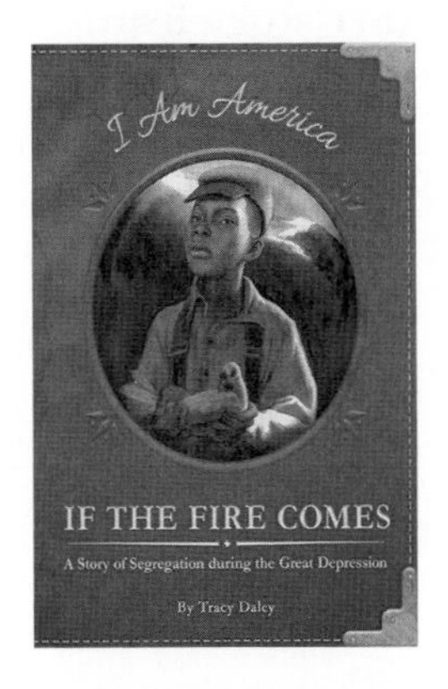

If the Fire Comes

A Story of Segregation during the Great Depression

By Tracy Daley
Illustrated by Eric Freeberg

☆ "The author's skillful blend of fact and fiction is backed up by fascinating backmatter . . . historical facts are woven into the story with such finesse readers will be eager to learn more."
—*Kirkus Reviews*, starred review for *If the Fire Comes*

Journey to a Promised Land

A Story of the Exodusters

By Allison Lassieur
Illustrated by Eric Freeberg

☆ "This well-written volume fills a major gap in historical fiction."
—*Kirkus Reviews*, starred review for *Journey to a Promised Land*

History is full of storytellers

Take a sneak peek at an excerpt from *If the Fire Comes: A Story of Segregation during the Great Depression* by Tracy Daley, another story from the I Am America series.

August 5, 1935
Mission: Save the Pigeons
Operative: Joseph McCoy

Summary:

It's been a week since I brought the pigeons home. They made Maya smile. The last few months since she's had polio have been hard. Her legs don't work right anymore, and she's been stuck in bed. There are two things that cheer her up: my spy stories and the presents I bring home—the pigeons being the best find so far.

I tell her the story every night to see if she'll smile again—how I knew the gambler, a pigeon racer, was down on his luck. I'd shined his shoes a dozen times, so I'd heard all his stories. I followed him five blocks without being noticed, sly as a real spy, and watched him dump his losing birds in the trash behind the mercantile.

Maya's favorite part is how I waited until he left and then saved the birds, bent cages and all.

I'd heard how pigeons can send messages, and I thought Maya and I could use them in our spy games, but something's wrong. The last few days, the pigeons have been lying down, not getting up when I bring them the leftover cornbread and milk. Maya says they are sick because we aren't feeding them right.

Today, I'm going to make enough money to get real pigeon feed. I might have to shine a dozen shoes to do it, but I'm not coming home until I can make the birds better. I worry that if something happens to the pigeons, Maya might never smile again.

Joseph McCoy could tell a lot by the shoes a person wore. Or didn't wear.

Uncle Tanner's shoes sat by the door of the shop Joseph and his family lived in, untouched on a weekday morning. Uncle Tanner's boots, a pair of Red Wings worn down to the metal over the toe, told the story of a man who'd worked hard once.

Shifting the boots to set his shoeshine box down by the door, Joseph could smell the oil and smoke from the leather. Uncle Tanner had been a metalworker before the Depression. He'd even been able to save up to have his own shop and tools, but he'd been out of work for almost two years now. His boots sat by the door more and more often. It was rare for Uncle Tanner to even come out of the back room now.

Joseph checked his shoeshine box, making sure his supplies were ready for the day: black liquid, polishing cloth, Griffin shoe polish, and several small brushes. Joseph was the best shoeshine in Elsinore, California. He knew how to get every detail right, and his hands didn't shake, steady and sure. He never got black on a customer's socks. Joseph could tell the difference between a movie star and an athlete, a businessman and a crook, or a banker and a lawyer.

"You leaving already?" Maya asked, making Joseph jump.

"I want to get an early start," Joseph said, walking across the shop to the side of Maya's bed. She slept out in the open; Joseph slept on the floor next to her. The shop only had one room in the back, where Uncle Tanner disappeared to more and more often.

Maya was two years older than Joseph, a ripe old age of thirteen, but she still liked to play their spy game. And even though she didn't get around the way she used to, she could talk all day, fix a clock without thinking, and pinch as hard as a crab.

Joseph was about to sit down next to her when he heard cooing coming from Maya's feet. Not again. He pulled the thin blanket up from the bottom and found Simon, Maya's favorite bird. He was nestled between

Maya's crooked legs, thin as pencils. He could see a spot of blood on her ankles from where she must have dragged her legs across the floor.

"Simon wasn't feeling well. I wanted to keep him warm," Maya said, sticking her chin out in her stubborn way.

"Are you okay?" Joseph asked.

"Of course," Maya said, but Joseph saw her tuck her hands behind her back. She got slivers when she dragged herself across the shop, no matter how many times Joseph swept. Maya was hard to keep down.

Joseph reached down and patted Simon, the smallest of the seventeen pigeons, on the head. Beside the bird, Joseph saw the book they read each night, *The Thirty-Nine Steps*, which had been one of Momma's favorite spy novels. It helped them get in the mood for their game and keep life exciting for Maya. Their game was to pretend Joseph was going out on a spy mission, a shoeshine boy as his cover.

Joseph wanted to say more about Maya pulling herself across the floor to get to the pigeon cages, but

Maya gave him one of her looks. She pushed herself up to a sitting position, hanging on to the side of the bed for support. "I'll check the radio, in case a secret message comes through. You go see what you can find out from the contacts downtown."

They kept the radio close to Maya's bed so she could listen during the day. She'd read all of Momma's spy novels at least ten times over. They usually had fun playing spies, but Maya didn't smile today, and her voice was flat. She was just trying to get him out of the shop.

"What can I bring you today?" Joseph asked. "Maybe some peanut butter and crackers?" They were Maya's favorite, and she needed something to look forward to.

Maya hadn't been the same since Momma's heart had given out two years ago. Papa had died from influenza when Joseph was small, so him being gone was just a fact of life. But Momma . . . well, Momma's absence had left a huge hole in both their hearts, Maya's especially.

Uncle Tanner was Momma's only brother, and he'd been kind and understanding at first. But after Uncle Tanner had lost his job, things had changed. They'd had to move out of Uncle Tanner's house and into the shop where he used to work. It was mostly cleaned out now, the tools sold to keep them fed. Uncle Tanner's kindness seemed to dwindle with the sale of each tool.

All that was left now was the forge with the bellows, a brass blowtorch, and some hand tools hanging along the wall. It wasn't a large shop, but the emptiness made the space feel hollow.

"I need some wheels," Maya said, lowering her head to the pillow. "Maybe a bike. Bring me a bike." She gave him a sad smile like she was sorry for asking. "And the crown jewels of England."

"I'm a spy, not a thief."

"Yes, of course," Maya said, turning her head away from him. "A war hero. Go spy me some peanut butter and crackers."

Joseph resolved to shine enough shoes to get the crackers, food for the birds, and maybe a treat to go with it.

He slipped out the door of the shop and blinked at the bright morning sun. The shop was the last building on the south side of town, which might have explained why no one had bothered to kick Uncle Tanner out. Joseph liked the space on the edge of town. The large field behind the shop was flat and open, providing a beautiful view of the mountains.

Joseph walked through Elsinore, a couple miles to the center of everything. It was where the new city hall stood, tall and glorious, red brick with a dozen windows, built just last year. Uncle Tanner had tried to get a job to help build the city hall, but they had been hiring whites only. The Depression had made whites so desperate for work they were taking jobs they never would have done before, jobs that black people used to do. Now there was no work at all. If a white man applied, he got it first. Uncle Tanner had complained long and loud for a while, but lately he hadn't even bothered to make a fuss.

City hall was where the shoes were. Politicians and bankers, lawyers and crooks all came to city hall. It helped that the bank was right across the street. There was a crowd outside today, a buzz of news in the air, the kind of news that starts small and then spreads like a wildfire. This was just the place for a spy.